DREAMW...

TROLLHUNTERS

TALES OF ARCADIA

FROM GUILLERMO DEL TORO

THE ADVENTURE BEGINS

Adapted by Richard Ashley Hamilton

Simon Spotlight

New York   London   Toronto   Sydney   New Delhi

SIMON SPOTLIGHT
An imprint of Simon & Schuster Children's Publishing Division
1230 Avenue of the Americas, New York, New York 10020
This Simon Spotlight edition December 2017
DreamWorks Trollhunters © 2017 DreamWorks Animation L.L.C. All Rights Reserved. All rights reserved, including the right of reproduction in whole or in part in any form. SIMON SPOTLIGHT and colophon are registered trademarks of Simon & Schuster, Inc. For information about special discounts for bulk purchases, please contact Simon & Schuster Special Sales at 1-866-506-1949 or business@simonandschuster.com.
Designed by Nick Sciacca
Manufactured in the United States of America 0218 OFF
10 9 8 7 6 5 4 3 2 1
ISBN 978-1-5344-1293-4 (hc)
ISBN 978-1-5344-1292-7 (pbk)
ISBN 978-1-5344-1294-1 (eBook)

ONE LAST HUNT

Kanjigar knew he was going to die exactly one day before it actually happened. The Amulet told him so.

He felt the device ticking on the armor over his heart, as it had done for centuries. Until yesterday, when it suddenly started ticking faster and louder than it ever had before. Like a countdown.

Tick. Tick. Tick.

In that moment Kanjigar knew this hunt would be his last. The realization didn't really surprise him. Countless Trolls had carried the Amulet before Kanjigar, so part of him always knew that he, too, would fall in battle one day. The Amulet would then call out for a new champion—the next Trollhunter— to carry out the unknowable wishes of its creator, Merlin the Wizard.

Crossing Heartstone Trollmarket, Kanjigar's underground home for the past two hundred years or so, he walked between caves bustling with thousands of Trolls of all shapes and sizes. Radiant gemstones reflected their neon colors across Kanjigar's engraved metal armor. He smiled at the massive Heartstone that towered over Trollmarket, filling its subterranean residents—Kanjigar included—with precious life energy. His smile faded, though, when he remembered that this would be his final visit to Trollmarket and that his energy would soon return to the Heartstone. With his remaining time, the Trollhunter knew that he must say good-bye to those who were closest to him.

Tick. Tick. Tick.

Kanjigar bowed his head so that his horns wouldn't scrape against the library entrance, as they had countless times before, carving twin grooves into the stone archway. Inside the library he found his two best friends, Blinkous Galadrigal and AAARRRGGHH!!!

"Why, if it isn't Kanjigar the Courageous," said Blinky, clapping all four of his hands together in delight. "To what do we owe this most prestigious of honors? If you're here to review *Gringold's Grimoire* again, I'm afraid I have it checked out to Vendel."

"That's quite all right, Blinky," said Kanjigar. "For I come in search of warm conversation, not dusty old books."

"I must say, that seems quite unlike you, Kanjigar," said Blinky. "Er, no offense."

"It's true," AAARRRGGHH!!! mumbled, lowering his horned head meekly. "Never talk anymore."

Kanjigar sat down beside the pair at the large reading table covered with numerous open volumes and research scrolls and sighed, "For that, I apologize, my friends. I have been distracted of late. The burdens of the Trollhunter weigh heavily on my mind. But now . . . now I'm finally remembering what is most important to me."

Blinky and AAARRRGGHH!!! traded a look of concern as Kanjigar considered the library around them. Thousands of leather-bound books and various relics from their past adventures crammed its shelves, including a large rusted propeller.

"Do you recall the time we tracked those Goblins to that human airfield on the surface?" Kanjigar asked with a grin.

"But of course!" said Blinky, his six eyes brightening at the memory. "Back in . . . 1942. On the human calendar, of course."

Kanjigar's grin spread to AAARRRGGHH!!! and Blinky as they shared his memory.

"My, how those Goblins tore apart those 'air-o-planes.' Pointless contraptions," Blinky continued. "Why would any sane creature possibly want to fly when they can remain perfectly safe underground? And those poor, frightened pilots! What did they call the Goblins when they saw them? 'Gromets'? 'Grammars'?"

"Gremlins," said AAARRRGGHH!!!

The three Trolls laughed so hard, Kanjigar almost forgot the Amulet.

Tick. Tick. Tick.

Kanjigar closed his eyes, exhaled, and stood up.

"The sun has set above," said Kanjigar. "I had best begin my patrol."

Blinky began, "Then let me gather my supplies so that AAARRRGGHH!!! and I might join—"

"That won't be necessary, old friend," Kanjigar interrupted. "Stay, both of you, and think more on old times."

"Kanjigar," said AAARRRGGHH!!! in a soft voice. "Everything . . . all right?"

The Trollhunter thought for a moment before he forced a weak smile at his enormous ally and said, "It will be."

Kanjigar then clapped AAARRRGGHH!!! and Blinky on their shoulders and left the library before they could ask anything else. He turned left at the Glug Pub and continued down the path to the Hero's Forge.

There, at the center of the sprawling arena, Draal trained. He dodged a razor-sharp pendulum, weaved between jets of fire, and tucked his body into a rolling, spiked ball to smash through a stone barrier. When the dust cleared, Draal looked up and saw Kanjigar at the sidelines. Their matching nose rings glinted in the faint gemlight.

"Most impressive," said Kanjigar, cocking his eyebrow.

"Thank you, Father," Draal answered. "Yet it pales in comparison to your mighty deeds."

"Draal, I—" Kanjigar began, unsure of what to say next.

He moved closer, wanting to share the pride he

felt for Draal . . . until he remembered the Amulet that occupied the space between his heart and his son.

Tick. Tick. Tick.

"Your guard," Kanjigar finally managed to say after changing his mind. "Remember to keep it up after you come out of a roll. To protect against a side attack."

"I shall, Father," Draal said dutifully before watching his father's armored form turn and leave him—and Trollmarket—for good.

Kanjigar still thought about Draal, Blinky, and AAARRRGGHH!!! hours later as he crept into the abandoned factory on the surface world. His armor shone in the moonlight that filtered through the broken windows. He trod lightly across shattered glass, wads of garbage, and a downed sign that said VESPA MOTORS ASSEMBLY PLANT in humanspeak, following a trail of blood drops.

Tick. Tick. Tick.

Hearing voices ahead, low and sinister, Kanjigar eased over to the corner and peered around. There, before him, the Trollhunter saw his prey: Bular, Son of Gunmar.

The massive red-eyed monster sat on a throne of discarded engine blocks and bent metal. At his cloven feet kneeled three reptilian Changelings: one tall and gaunt male, one squat and bearded male, and one lithe female with menace flashing in her eyes.

"You have heard my father's orders, Impures," said Bular with a snarl. "Hasten your search. The time of Gunmar's return draws near."

"As you wish, O Great Bular," said the gaunt one with a hint of sarcasm. "But might I point out that we're not alone?"

Bular's head whipped up and a growl formed in his throat as Kanjigar walked into the makeshift throne room.

"Merlin's creation," sneered Bular.

"You've grown sloppy in your arrogance, Bular," said Kanjigar. "Even a blind Nyarlagroth could have followed that blood trail."

The throne shuddered with a metal-on-metal screech as Bular rose. The three Changelings got to their feet and instinctively backed into the shadows.

"A Troll has to eat, and there are so many

delicious fleshbags to choose from on the surface," Bular said with a terrifying smile.

Bular unsheathed the two swords from his back and leaped off his throne, his powerful legs carrying him across the entire factory floor. Kanjigar held out his hand, and his broadsword, Daylight, manifested instantaneously. Swinging his weapon like a club, Kanjigar smacked Bular with the flat of the blade, sending him crashing through the building's crumbling brick walls.

Tick. Tick. Tick.

Kanjigar followed outside, only for Bular to reach out from the darkness with a roar. His claw grabbed the Trollhunter by the helmet and tossed him bodily into a nearby neighborhood. The two warriors tussled down the streets, smashing into mailboxes, setting off car alarms, and slicing through trees with their weapons.

With his eye swelling from a bruise, Kanjigar glanced up at the sky. The horizon turned from purple to orange with the coming sunrise.

Tick. Tick. Tick.

Bular lunged at Kanjigar. The Trollhunter sidestepped the attack, letting Bular's momentum carry him tumbling down a concrete ramp. The dark Troll came to a stop in the dry canal that ran through this human town, Arcadia Oaks. Kanjigar charged after Bular, their swords clashing again under a looming bridge crossing the canal above them.

"Yield, Kanjigar!" thundered Bular, his body heaving from exertion.

"A Trollhunter never yields," said Kanjigar, equally spent. "I'd rather die."

"Terms accepted," said Bular.

So focused was Kanjigar on his nemesis that he failed to notice the sun rising above him. A beam of light glanced off the Trollhunter's armor, turning one of its corners to lifeless stone.

Bular used the distraction to kick Daylight out of the Trollhunter's grip. Kanjigar scrambled after his weapon, but he recoiled when another shaft of sunlight appeared between his fingers and the sword. He felt his hand go numb and the Amulet's glow start to fade.

Tick. Tick. Tick.

The Trollhunter bounded for the bridge and climbed up, around, and below its weathered struts. But Bular followed. Kanjigar ignored his taunts and the hot, rotted meat stench of his breath as the evil Troll pinned him to the bridge's edge. Bular forced Kanjigar's face into the sunlight, burning half of it into dead, unmoving stone.

Kanjigar heard himself scream, but it sounded distant to him. Summoning the last of his strength, he clasped his hand around Bular's forearm and yanked it into the sunlight as well. Bular howled in agony, but all Kanjigar could hear was the incessant ticking of the Amulet, the countdown nearing its end. Soon it would all be over.

Tick.

Regaining his footing on the brink, Kanjigar found himself trapped between his enemy and the risen sun. Bular pulled out his swords again, albeit with a bit more trouble due to his now-paralyzed claw.

Tick.

"It's me or the sun," said Bular. "Either way, you're doomed."

Tick.

"No," said Kanjigar with difficulty. "The Amulet will find a champion. We will stop you and your master. I may end, but the fight will not."

The Amulet stopped ticking. A sense of peace washed over Kanjigar as he folded his arms across his chest, secure in the knowledge of what he needed to do next. With one simple step backward, Kanjigar fell off the bridge and into pure, golden sunlight.

"Please, Merlin, let your Amulet choose anyone other than my son," whispered the Trollhunter a second before his stone body shattered upon impact with the ground.

CHAPTER 1
DAYLIGHT

The alarm clock on the desk clicked to 6:00 a.m., emitting the same annoying beep it did every school day. James Lake Jr. blinked his eyes open slowly, still remembering his strange dream. He was surrounded by thousands of disassembled Vespa scooter parts without instructions or anyone around to help him put it all back together. And Jim had this feeling that carried over from the dream into the morning—a dreadful sense that time was running out. Looking at the alarm clock didn't help the feeling go away.

Dressing and combing his black hair in a hurry, Jim went downstairs into the kitchen and started cooking three meals at once: buttered toast for himself (a simple but oh-so-satisfying breakfast), a chipotle-ketchup-glazed meat loaf baking in the oven, and a caramelized onion and goat cheese omelet. Jim worked his Santoku knife with practiced precision across the cutting board, putting a fine dice on the red onions. And he had enough faded scars on his fingertips to remind him to keep them tucked as he sliced the basil into a chiffonade.

Multitasking around the kitchen, Jim pulled the meat loaf from the oven and portioned three slices of it into three separate sandwiches, and folded the omelet effortlessly in the skillet. Not bad for a Tuesday. Now came Jim's favorite part: he washed his knife in the sink and air-dried it by twirling the blade between his fingers.

Kids, don't try this at home, Jim thought. Unless your mom works crazy-long hours and you've gotten totally sick of eating PB and J alone every night.

Once he had spun every last drop of moisture off its surface, Jim holstered the Santoku in the knife block, plated the omelet, and carried it upstairs on a tray. He gently opened the door to the second bedroom and found his mom, Barbara, sound asleep in her bed.

Jim set the tray down on the night table, gently removed his mom's glasses from her face, and polished them with his sweater before placing them next to the omelet. Seeing her there, looking so peaceful, Jim felt kind of sorry for his mom. She worked so hard at the hospital, actually saving peoples' lives, and providing for the two of them. Jim vowed long ago never to complain about making meals. It was the least he could do to help his mom out. That, and she was also a really terrible cook.

"Love you, Mom," Jim said softly as he kissed her on the head and went back downstairs.

The garage door cranked open mechanically, and Jim walked his bike outside, squinting against the brilliant sunlight.

"We're late for school, Jimbo," called a familiar voice.

Jim smiled when he saw Toby Domzalski waiting for him at the end of the driveway. Tobes was trying to stuff his head into a bike helmet that he had long since outgrown.

"Sorry, Tobes," said Jim. "Busy with the lunches. One for me, one for Mom, and . . ."

Jim held out a brown paper bag, and Toby eagerly snatched it, inhaling deeply.

"Ah," Toby sighed. "Balsamic mushrooms, meat loaf—chunky—sun-dried tomatoes . . ."

Toby's braces shined in the sunlight as he rolled his tongue inside his mouth, trying to place that last flavor he was smelling.

"And cardamom," said Jim.

"Ooh, taking a chance there, Chef Jim!" Toby replied.

Jim smiled. Ever since kindergarten, Toby had always had, well, an appreciation for food. Toby loved the way Jim used equal parts ground beef and pork to keep his meat loaf tender, and Jim loved how Toby loved stuff like that.

"What's life without a little adventure?" joked Jim as he hopped onto his bike.

Toby did the same (after a few failed attempts), and the guys pedaled their way to school. Since they were running late, they cut through the woods toward the canal to save five minutes. Toby complained about the bumpy ride, but Jim couldn't help but tune him out a bit and savor the ride. He lived for moments like these—racing against the clock, feeling the wind against his face, and jumping his bike over a hill whenever he got a chance.

Those little thrills kept Jim focused on the moment and not worried about the day ahead. The idea of sitting through a bunch of classes he was not particularly good at, all while trying not to stare at the amazing girl who didn't even know he existed, made Jim's stomach twist. He wondered how long he would feel this way. How long he would just be so . . . ordinary. All through high school? College? That sensation of time running out returned to Jim, sending a fresh pang of worry to his gut.

Oh well, Jim thought as Toby blabbed on behind him. *Claire Nuñez may never notice me, but at least I've got Tobes. And my mom. And a promising career making sandwiches, I guess. Meat loaf is great and all, but still. I wish there was . . . more.*

Jim tried to push all his anxiety aside as he rushed toward the canal. Reaching its concrete edge, Jim pulled up on his handlebars and his bike caught air. During the downward arc, he felt free—free of responsibility, free of worry, free of that nagging voice in his head—for a few fun, fleeting, glorious seconds.

The tires landed at the bottom of the canal with a rubber squeak, and Jim looked back toward the woods, waiting for the lagging Toby.

"Come on, Tobes!" Jim called out, his voice bouncing against the canal's graffiti-covered walls.

No response came from Toby. He was probably too far behind to hear Jim anyway. Instead, Jim heard another voice echo in his mind. Not the usual one that popped up to second-guess Jim all the time.

No, this was an unfamiliar voice. It sounded old, powerful, and deathly serious as Jim felt it call out his name.

"James Lake."

CHAPTER 2
CHOSEN

"Curse this infernal sunlight!" shouted Blinky.

His four hands rattled the corroded metal grate of the drain tunnel before him, but it did not budge. AAARRRGGHH!!! hunched behind Blinky and winced at the noise, his eyes welling with tears. For both Trolls had watched from this dark hiding spot in the dry canal as their best friend, Kanjigar, sacrificed himself mere hours ago.

Blinky and AAARRRGGHH!!! had each felt unsettled after Kanjigar left the library of Troll lore. Something about what he'd said—or hadn't said— and the way the Trollhunter's eyes wouldn't quite meet their own, had concerned both of them. So when Kanjigar was late in returning home from his nightly patrol, Blinky and AAARRRGGHH!!! traveled from Heartstone Trollmarket to that drain tunnel on the surface world.

As the sun broke through the morning fog, the two Trolls caught the very last of Kanjigar's final battle with Bular. AAARRRGGHH!!! could have very easily knocked the grate aside with his tremendous strength, but burning sunlight had filled the canal between their tunnel and the bridge. Blinky cried out at the top of his lungs to try to distract Bular. But the bridge was too far away. And so the two Trolls watched in horror as the Trollhunter plunged off the bridge and smashed against the canal floor into thousands of shards of rock.

AAARRRGGHH!!! had to look away after that, but Blinky derived some grim satisfaction in spying on Bular as the dark Troll tried in vain to reach the Amulet buried within Kanjigar's remains. Every time Bular neared the pile of rubble, the rays of sunlight that surrounded it would sear his stone skin. After several failed attempts and enraged roars of frustration—and the human city now waking up around him—Bular finally retreated into the nearby woods, which were still untouched by the morning sun. For the longest time after that, Blinky and AAARRRGGHH!!! did not speak to each other. They just sat there, in the dank and musty tunnel, wordlessly heartbroken.

"Why?" Blinky uttered in a hoarse whisper. "Why would Kanjigar not accept our assistance when we offered it earlier? Perhaps if I'd been more forceful in my—"

"No," grumbled AAARRRGGHH!!!. "Kanjigar wanted it this way."

"But . . . why?" Blinky had to ask again.

The question vexed him, and his six eyebrows were arched in confusion, until he heard a new sound over the faint trickle of sewer water. Looking past the grate and into the canal, Blinky spotted a human boy on his—oh, what were they called again? Ah, yes—bicycle. The boy removed his helmet and massaged his temples as if fighting off a headache.

A larger boy soon joined the first in the canal, though he appeared to be in far less control of his bicycle. Screaming his head off, he sped down the canal's incline, passed his friend, rolled backward, and fell flat on his face.

"HA! How awesome are we?" Blinky heard the large one groan as he lifted himself off the concrete, raising a feeble thumbs-up. "We are awesome!"

AAARRRGGHH!!! was roused by the commotion and looked over Blinky's shoulder at the two young humans. In silence, the Trolls watched the dark-haired boy drop his helmet carelessly to the side. He took an uncertain step toward what was left of Kanjigar, then another.

"Great Gronka Morka," Blinky uttered in a hushed voice.

"You said it," AAARRRGGHH!!! whispered back.

"JAMES LAKE."

The voice in Jim's head was growing so loud, he thought his skull would split open. He took off his helmet to relieve the pressure and stumbled forward. Somehow, moving in that direction lessened the intensity of the voice. Jim took another step, and the voice grew quieter still. Looking ahead, Jim discovered a pile of rubble at the center of the canal, just below the bridge.

"JAMES LAKE," the voice called again.

"Hey, Tobes," Jim called over his shoulder as he kneeled in front of the rock pile. "Did you hear that voice?"

"What voice?" Toby asked, catching up to Jim and peering down at the shattered stones.

Great, Jim thought. *Now I'm imagining voices that only I can hear. Guess I can add insanity to my unpopularity and rotten grade point average.*

"JAMES LAKE," the voice called from within the rocks. It was so loud, both Jim and Toby fell backward in surprise.

The two friends exchanged a spooked look. On the one hand, Jim was happy that Toby heard it too. That meant Jim wasn't crazy. Or that the craziness might be contagious and they'd both wind up in a hospital. At least they'd be together. . . .

But on the other hand, stones weren't supposed to speak directly into a person's brain.

"That," Jim managed to say. "That—that—that pile of rocks knows my name!"

The guys inched closer to the rubble. Jim eyed it warily, but Toby shrugged.

"It's a pile of K-spar. Minerals don't talk," Toby said. If there was one thing he enjoyed almost as much as Jim's cooking, it was geology.

The voice had stopped ringing in Jim's head, yet he still felt like he was being somehow . . .

compelled. His hand reached into the pile of rocks, almost against his will.

"There's gotta be a walkie-talkie in here or something," Toby said, just as Jim's fingers brushed against a smooth and cool object underneath the stones. But it sure didn't feel like any walkie-talkie.

Jim removed his hand from the rubble. Uncurling his fingers, he discovered a large circular gadget in his palm, almost like an oversized stopwatch, but made from some shimmering metal he didn't recognize. Holding it closer, Jim studied its intricate gears, its etchings, and the odd foreign words that had been carved into its back.

"Huh," Jim said. "Looks like . . . an amulet."

Still hidden in the drainpipe, Blinky and AAARRRGGHH!!! stared at each other when they heard the boy say "amulet."

Truth be told, Toby had been the victim of numerous practical jokes during his childhood, and this whole thing with the rocks and the voice all screamed "prank" to him. He looked up to the bridge and yelled, "Who's doing this? Come out now!"

Blinky and AAARRRGGHH!!! instinctively backed

away from the grate. Meanwhile, Jim held the mysterious Amulet closer to his ear.

"Hello?" he said to it. "I'm listening."

Jim closed his eyes, expecting that voice to return and maybe say something other than his name for the umpteenth time, when . . .

RIIIIINNNNNGGGGG!

Jim and Toby both froze at the distant sound. They knew it all too well.

"Ugh! Final bell!" Toby said. "We're so late, our kids are gonna have detention!"

Without a second thought, Jim pocketed the Amulet in his book bag, snapped on his helmet, hopped onto his bike, and said, "Come on, Tobes! We can still make it!"

"I'm right behind!" Toby replied as he and Jim hustled past the drainage tunnel and toward their high school.

Once the sounds of the boys' tires had faded away, Blinky and AAARRRGGHH!!! returned to the grate.

"It chose . . . a human!" said Blinky, his many eyes all wide with disbelief.

CHAPTER 3
GYM CLASS ZEROES

Jim and Toby skidded to a halt in front of the bike racks and locked their tires into place. Fortunately, a few other students were still straggling into Arcadia Oaks High School after the final bell.

"Baby wipe?" said Toby, offering Jim a moist towelette from his overstuffed backpack.

"Um, no thanks?" Jim replied.

"Suit yourself," Toby said as he wiped the sweat from his face and under his arms. "But after a vigorous bike ride like that, I want to smell my best for the ladies."

Toby saw Darci Scott and Mary Wang hurrying up the school's front steps. He pointed two fingers at them, winked, and called out, "'Sup, future girlfriends?"

"As if, Dumbzalski," Mary hissed.

"Hear that, Jimbo?" Toby asked with a smile. "They're actually talking to me now. We're making progress!"

Normally, Jim was amazed by Toby's endless supply of self-confidence. But today all he could think about was that Amulet in his bag. Had it really called to him? But why? Why him, of all people?

Jim was about to reach for the Amulet when he froze in place. He saw an SUV pull up to the school, a BABY ON BOARD decal hanging from its rear window. The passenger door opened, and out she stepped.

Claire Nuñez.

That freedom-slash-falling feeling Jim had had earlier on his bike? It came back stronger than ever as Claire waved good-bye to her mom and sprinted past him into Arcadia Oaks High School. Jim could still smell her perfume in the air.

"Gardenias," Jim said dreamily to nobody in particular.

"Ah, Jimbo?" Toby said. "You feeling okay, buddy? You look a little woozy."

Jim didn't bother to answer. He was still thinking about Claire, his mind reeling back to the first time he'd laid eyes on her. It was last year, at a City Council fund-raiser held at the hospital. As a doctor on staff, Barbara was invited to attend, and she brought Jim as her plus one. Jim dreaded going. What if someone from school—like, say, Steve Palchuk—saw Jim on a date with his mom? But those worries melted away when Barbara and Jim were introduced to the party's host, Councilwoman Nuñez, and her daughter, Claire.

As the moms talked about how Claire was transferring from a prep school to Arcadia Oaks High School, Jim couldn't help but stare. Claire was obviously very pretty. But there seemed to be more to her than just surface looks. Jim stared as Claire tugged at the party dress that was probably as uncomfortable on her as the rented tux was on Jim. And he kept staring when Claire, clearly bored, requested a song from the DJ, then rocked out all by herself on the dance floor to the latest Papa Skull single.

And Jim was still staring at Claire today, admiring the back of her head in their AP World History class. Suddenly he came to and looked around.

AP World History?! How did I get here? Jim

wondered, since he didn't remember walking into the classroom, sitting down, or opening his laptop at all. *Oh my God, have I just been staring at Claire this entire time? She must think I'm some sort of dweeb or—*

"Close your mouth," whispered Toby, who was seated right beside Jim in class. "You're drooling."

"No. No, I'm not," said Jim, finally snapping out of it and finding Toby typing on his laptop. "What're you doing?"

"Research," Toby whispered.

"Hey, look up 'talking Amulet,'" Jim joked quietly.

Toby rolled his eyes. "I already did that. All I got was toys. One of 'em was a plushie!"

Jim looked over Toby's shoulder at the laptop screen and, sure enough, the search engine had turned up lots of pictures of colorful toys, but nothing that even remotely resembled the Amulet in his book bag. The guys were so engrossed in what they were seeing that their teacher, Walter Strickler, couldn't help but notice.

Without missing a beat, Mr. Strickler continued talking about the Peloponnesian War, walked up the boys' aisle, and said, "Jim, would you agree?"

Busted, Jim looked up at his teacher and blurted out a confused, "Sir?"

Mr. Strickler said something else, but Jim couldn't understand it. All he could think about was the other kids in class all snickering at him. Jim replied to his teacher, but he didn't know what he was saying. It was like he was on some sort of spastic autopilot. His cheeks flushed red and he started feeling warm all around his collar.

Oh no, Jim fretted. *Claire must think I'm such a loser! I bet she's laughing along with everyone else and—*

Another bell rang, signaling the end of class. As the other students got up and collected their belongings, Jim averted his eyes and grabbed his bag. Maybe he could sneak out unnoticed.

"Jim, may I have a word?" Mr. Strickler asked after the other kids had left.

Jim flinched and dropped his bag, spilling most of its contents—books, pencils, headphones, but not the Amulet, fortunately. How would he explain that to his teacher on top of spacing out in his class?

Mr. Strickler helped Jim pick up his things and said, "Jim, you're distracted."

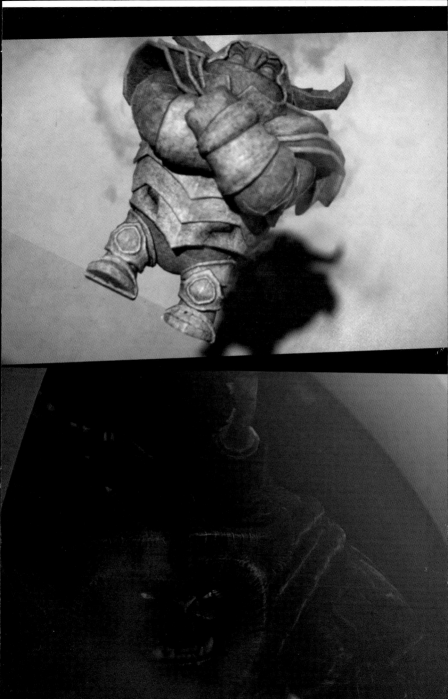

"Sorry," Jim said as he stood up. "I didn't get a lot of sleep last night."

Strickler nodded in understanding and said, "I know it's just you and your mother, and you want to help her—"

"She's just really tired, Mr. Strickler," Jim interrupted. "She's been working double shifts at the clinic."

"I believe I'm long overdue for a conversation with her," Mr. Strickler said, clicking his pen and jotting his number on a sticky note. "Have her call me, please. And feel free to drop by my office if you ever need to talk."

Jim took Mr. Strickler's number and muttered, "Yeah, I'll do that."

Slinging his bag over his shoulder, Jim turned to leave.

"Oh, and Jim," Mr. Strickler said with a wink, "if you fancy Miss Nuñez, I submit that talking to will be much more effective than staring at."

Jim smiled awkwardly and slinked out of the classroom, leaving Mr. Strickler alone with his thoughts.

For some reason, Mr. Strickler had always felt there was something special about Jim Lake. He certainly wasn't the best student in class, but Walter Strickler had been living and teaching in Arcadia Oaks for a very long time. And he knew potential when he saw it.

Mr. Strickler's advice stayed with Jim throughout the next period: PE. At first Jim had thought he was going to get the scolding of a lifetime, but ol' Walter actually went pretty easy on him. And Jim couldn't argue with Mr. Strickler's logic. Obviously, he was a smart guy, and he generally seemed to look out for Jim. And, hey, Strickler was reasonably in shape, well dressed, and, y'know, handsome for his age. This was a man who definitely put some thought into his appearance. He probably did okay in the dating department. So maybe he was right about Jim just going up and talking to Claire.

Why not? Jim thought. *Today's already been full of miracles. Found an Amulet. Didn't get a tardy notice. Toby actually climbed the rope.*

It was true. Sort of. Toby still dangled about two feet above the ground on the rope suspended from the gymnasium rafters—a new personal best. The only downside was that Toby still had about eight more feet to climb. And he was hanging upside down.

Jim spotted Claire on the bleachers across the basketball court, hanging out with Mary and Darci. Straightening his gym uniform, he marched over to the girls like a man on a mission. Along the way, Jim figured that maybe he should've taken Toby up on that baby wipe, but, well, it was too late for that now. Jim was sure he saw Claire look up and glance at him before returning her attention to whatever funny video they were watching on Mary's phone.

He reached the bleachers, took a deep breath, and said, of all things, *"Buenas noches."*

YOU IDIOT! screamed the old, questioning voice in Jim's head, but it was too late. All three girls were staring at him.

"You . . . speak Spanish?" asked Claire.

Definitely not! Jim thought. *Maybe if I paid more attention to Señor Uhl in Spanish class than to that dyed-blue streak in your dark, lustrous hair!*

But all that really came out of Jim's mouth was "Uh . . . uh . . ."

"C'mon, Claire," said Darci as she and Mary stood to break the awkwardness.

Claire got up to follow them, but she paused and asked, "Do you like Shakespeare?"

"Um . . . what?" Jim said back.

Claire pulled a flyer from her notebook and handed it to Jim. It featured the famous balcony image from *Romeo and Juliet*.

"The school play," said Claire. "We're having trouble getting boys to audition."

She smiled at Jim, tucked her dyed-blue lock of hair behind her ear, and turned to rejoin her friends.

Jim couldn't help himself. He just had to say, *"Hasta huevo."*

With her back turned to Jim, Claire enjoyed a private smile. She'd been wanting to talk to him ever since they'd met briefly at one of her mom's countless boring fund-raisers. Seeing Jim get his mom some punch and even dance with her . . . Well, Claire didn't really meet guys who were that sweet at her old prep school. Other than that, and the fact that his Spanish definitely needed some work, Claire didn't know too much about Jim Lake.

But she wanted to.

CHAPTER 4

A FIRST TIME FOR EVERYTHING

AAARRRGGHH!!! dropped another toppling stack of scrolls onto the library's slab of a table, sending clouds of dust and loose pages everywhere.

"Thank you, Aarghaumont," said Blinky as he simultaneously scanned two different books with his four hands and six eyes, turning the pages frantically. "Now, if you could please find *Axle's Forbidden Almanac—*"

"Almond snack?" AAARRRGGHH!!! said in confusion.

"*Almanac,*" corrected Blinky, still reading at a fast clip. "It's an annual record of important dates, statistics, and tables."

Misunderstanding, AAARRRGGHH!!! lifted up one side of the incredibly heavy reading table in search of this almanac, causing all of Blinky's books and scrolls to slide off and fall to the ground.

"Oops," grumbled AAARRRGGHH!!!.

Blinky sighed, rubbed his many strained eyes, and said, "No matter, AAARRRGGHH!!!. I've double-checked all forty-seven volumes of *A Brief Recapitulation of Troll Lore* and have confirmed that every previous Trollhunter was, in fact, a Troll. It appears this—this—"

Blinky searched for a word until AAARRRGGHH!!! helpfully guessed, "Jimmy?"

"Yes, this Jimmy truly is the first human to ever inherit the mantle of Trollhunter," finished Blinky. "And he could not be in more danger."

"Bular," said AAARRRGGHH!!!.

"Correct. With the son of Gunmar still on the loose and in search of the Amulet for reasons unknown, the human stands to meet as violent and gruesome a fate as our dear, departed Kanjigar," said Blinky, more dread creeping into his voice with each word. "We must find this boy and train him before it's too—"

"Did you say something about Kanjigar?" asked a voice behind Blinky and AAARRRGGHH!!!.

They turned and found Draal at the library's entrance, a look of concern apparent on his normally serious face.

"What news have you about my father?" Draal continued. "He was due back from his hunt hours ago."

AAARRRGGHH!!! and Blinky traded a sad and uncomfortable look. In their grief and haste to return to Trollmarket and figure out what to do with this human chosen by the Amulet, they had completely neglected to tell Draal about Kanjigar.

Blinky stood, cleared his throat, and said, "Draal, I—we—must regrettably inform you that our Trollhunter, Kanjigar the Courageous . . . was felled in battle."

Draal's wide mouth opened slightly. His eyes searched Blinky's, then AAARRRGGHH!!!'s, and saw the truth in them. With a long, shuddering breath, Draal lowered his head, and his rocky shoulders sagged.

"Died . . . a hero," AAARRRGGHH!!! added softly.

"Yes, his sacrifice was a valiant one," said Blinky. "Thanks to your noble father, the Amulet is still safe, though inaccessible at the moment—"

Upon hearing the word "Amulet," Draal's eyes widened. He blinked away his tears and stood upright again, as if filled with new purpose.

"Then I must return to my training," Draal said, his voice building. "As the son of the greatest Trollhunter who ever lived, the Amulet will surely select me as his successor. Draal the Deadly will don his father's armor and visit revenge upon his killer!"

With that, Draal turned and left for the Hero's Forge before Blinky and AAARRRGGHH!!! could stop him. The two friends exchanged another troubled look.

"Great Gronka Morka?" AAARRRGGHH!!! guessed Blinky was going to say.

"Precisely," said Blinky.

Miles above Heartstone Trollmarket, the late afternoon sun cast long shadows across the dry canal, stretching from the bridge to the nearby woods. A pair of burning red eyes peered from between the darkened trees, followed by a low, guttural snarl. Bular, Son of Gunmar emerged, his mammoth body snapping branches with each plodding step.

He moved into the canal, sticking to the shadow

path that protected him from the sun. With his sword Bular prodded at Kanjigar's remains, searching for the Amulet, only to find it . . . missing. His eyes narrowed to glowing slits as he held his snout to the debris and sniffed, picking up a scent.

"Human," he uttered before releasing a fearsome war cry. Bular punched his stone fist against one of the bridge struts so hard, the motorists driving above thought they had just experienced a small earthquake.

CHAPTER 5
TICK-TOCK

Jim changed out of his gym clothes, trying not to gag at the sharp body odor and spray-on deodorant that filled the locker room. Toby sat on the bench beside him, struggling to put on his socks. Unfortunately, the formfitting pants his nana had bought for him weren't really letting Toby bend his knees.

"So close," Toby grunted. "You talked to her?"

"Yep," said Jim, looking around. He and Tobes were the last guys in the locker room—which was probably a good thing, because Toby accidentally slipped off the bench, fell backward, and banged his head into a locker with a resounding metal clang.

"Like, actually spoke to her?" asked Toby, apparently unharmed by the head injury. "Not just, you know, in your head?"

"I unleashed my español on her," Jim said. He opened his book bag and found the Amulet still tucked inside.

"You should totally do it," said Toby, now upright, an idea forming in his mind.

"What? The play?" Jim said. "I'm not an actor."

Toby struggled with the sock again and said, with effort, "Come on. You're always saying how you want your life to be more exciting. Right?"

"I don't think *Romeo and Juliet* is exactly the answer, Tobes," Jim said, considering the Amulet in his hand. "I don't mean just, you know, exciting. I mean . . ."

He studied his reflection on the Amulet's polished surface, his face appearing warped by the tiny inscriptions in the metal. Jim hardly recognized the person staring back at him.

"More," Jim finished. "I just need to know that there's something more to life than high school."

Out of the corner of his eye Jim glimpsed a sudden, dark movement. He quickly returned the Amulet to his bag and looked down to the end of the row of benches, but he saw nothing there.

"Something more?" Toby asked. That sock was

putting up so much of a fight, he was oblivious to a rattling sound that came from the other side of the lockers.

But Jim heard it. He left Toby with his socks and tight pants and followed the rattling around the corner. Thick steam billowed from the shower room just beyond him.

"Hello?" Jim said. "Anybody in there?"

Sometimes the other guys in gym class forgot to turn off the showers, wasting gallons of water despite the recent drought. Normally, Jim would hear their voices echoing off the tiled walls as they joked and whipped towels at one another.

But right now the shower room was silent except for the faint hiss of the water.

"Hello?" Jim said again, getting closer to the shower room, his pulse quickening.

If he had left the Amulet in his hand, Jim would have noticed how the glass pane on its front started glowing blue. Like a warning. But the Amulet remained in his bag, and Jim stepped into the shower room, his sneakers squeaking against the wet floor.

Jim could feel his heart beating in his chest. His eyes were straining to see past all the steam when a shape skittered across the far end of the showers and ducked into a stall.

Jim gasped as a loud holler came from behind him.

"Got one! Woo-hoo!" Toby yelled triumphantly, admiring the sock now pulled onto his foot.

Jim rolled his eyes, feeling silly for being so scared of a shower room. He turned on his heel and went back to Toby, shaking his head.

After Jim and Toby left together, Blinky stepped out from the shower stall, the hair on the back of his head wet and messy. He had heard enough from this Jimbo to understand he had no idea of the danger in which he had been placed. Now it would just be a matter of isolating the boy so that Blinky could speak to him alone, Troll to human, and begin his training in earnest. . . .

"So, good news, dude," Toby said as he and Jim walked their bicycles from the bike rack to the exit at the end of the day. "My orthodontist says I'm almost done with my braces. Only four more years!"

Toby smiled proudly, revealing a mouth full of complicated and painful-looking metal. But Jim had his head turned, looking across the campus to the breezeway, where Steve Palchuk was up to his usual antics. With his perfect blond hair, bulging muscles, and popped shirt collar, Steve always rubbed Jim the wrong way. And the fact that he was currently stuffing their frail classmate, Eli Pepperjack, into a locker sure didn't help.

Toby followed Jim's stare and said, "Okay, nothing to see here."

"We can't just let him do that," Jim replied, feeling his anger rise at the injustice.

"Oh, yes, we can. If Steve's terrorizing Eli, he's not terrorizing us," Toby said, still feeling the atomic wedgie Steve had given him last week. It hurt like blazes, yet Toby marveled at how his underwear waistband stretched all the way up and over his own head like that.

But the part of his brain that made Jim feel like time was running out also chimed in during situations like these. Jim might be a nobody, but how could anybody let something like this happen to a fellow human being?

Jim marched over to the breezeway far more confidently than he had marched up to Claire in the gymnasium. He arrived just in time to hear Steve pound on the locker door and taunt Eli.

"Tell me again, dweeb face," Steve said with a smirk. "Tell me about the creatures, and maybe I'll let you out!"

A few of Steve's cronies had gathered around and laughed at Eli's predicament. Jim felt his heart rate rise. That was happening a lot today.

"Or you can let him out right now," Jim blurted out. "I mean, you know, it would be nice."

Steve wheeled around, shot a dirty look at Jim, and said, "Nice would be you minding your own business."

But it was too late for that. Jim stood his ground. Behind him, Toby and some of the other students started to stare in their direction.

"Oh, hi, Jim!" called Eli, his voice muffled from inside the locker.

Steve slapped the locker again and said in a mock-casual voice, "So, where were we? Um . . . oh yeah, okay. You were telling me about the monsters you saw this morning, with fangs and—what was it again?"

"Stone for skin!" Eli said, his voice cracking with nerves. "In the canal!"

Stone? Canal? The words struck Jim, making his mind drift back to this morning and the Amulet.

He could still feel the weight of it in his bag. Was this a coincidence or . . . ?

"Stone for skin?" Steve chuckled. "Man, Eli, you've got some imagination!"

Jim's mind returned to the present. He parked his bike and looked Steve in the eye.

"Look, Steve, seriously," Jim said, his tone even. "Just let him out."

Steve moved so fast, Jim didn't even have time to react. The bully stepped forward, grabbed Jim by his book bag strap, and pulled him close. With his free hand, Steve cocked a meaty fist.

"Or you'll do what?" Steve said.

"Okay. Do it. Punch me," said Jim, the words just tumbling out of his mouth. At least they weren't in Spanish.

Steve blinked at Jim, not following him. His mouth hung open in confusion before he asked, "You . . . you're asking for a beating?"

"Yeah. Just go crazy," Jim answered. His arms remained at his sides, even as Steve's fist loomed before him. "In twenty years you're gonna be a nobody, and Eli will have a career in software and he'll be a billionaire."

The color drained from Toby's face. Clearly, Jim had gone crazy-town banana-pants.

"I do like computers!" Eli volunteered helpfully.

Steve finally swung his fist—not at Jim, but at the locker, his knuckles bashing into the metal door like a gong. That shut Eli up. Now Steve balled his fist again and aimed it at Jim. Jim shut his eyes, bracing for the worst, while Toby's brain raced in a panic.

"Let him out!" said Toby, looking expectantly at the other students around him. "Let him out!"

Some of the other kids repeated after Toby. "Let him out!"

They said it again and again, a chant forming.

"Let him out! Let him out! Let him out!"

One of Jim's eyes cracked open. Had Steve hit him so hard he was hearing things again? But no, Steve gaped at the chanting students around him, unsure of what to do.

"Palchuk!" yelled Coach Lawrence. He stood at the end of the breezeway, his whistle dangling around his thick neck. "What's going on here?"

Steve instantly released Jim, lowered his fist, and said unconvincingly, "Uh, nothing, sir."

"Why aren't you at practice?" the coach demanded.

"I was helping Eli here," lied Steve, indicating the locker. "He was stuck!"

"Hey, guys!" Eli said. He sounded positively cheerful inside the locker.

Coach Lawrence jerked a thumb to the school's sports field and barked, "On the double! Now!"

As soon as the coach's back was turned, Steve leaned in close and stared daggers at Jim.

"Friday at noon," Steve said in a low voice. "You and me."

Steve backed toward the field while wagging his finger back and forth at Jim like a metronome.

"Tick-tock," said Steve, his words dripping with menace. "Tick-tock."

And just like that, Jim felt like his time was running out all over again. His stomach clenched. He thought he could taste bile at the back of his throat.

Jim stood rooted in place, not even flinching when Eli tumbled out of the locker beside him.

"Thank you!" Eli said to Jim from the ground.

"Don't mention it," Jim said as he walked away. Right now he had bigger problems to worry about than a kid stuffed in a locker.

CHAPTER 6
PLEASE LET IT BE RACCOONS

Tick-tock. Tick-tock.

The threat of Steve Palchuk's revenge weighed on Jim the whole bike ride home. Not even the tangerine glow of the sunset or Toby's constant chatter could rouse Jim from his worries.

"That was awesome, man! Did you see how I did that chant?" Toby said, still thrilled with himself. "'Let him out! Let him out!' I mean, you probably won't live past Friday, but it was awesome."

Right. Awesome, thought Jim. *The promise of an upcoming pounding from Steve, the fact that Claire still probably has no idea who I am, plus homework, making tomorrow's meals . . . My life's just one big puddle of awesomesauce.*

"Hey, boys," called a warm voice.

Jim slowed to a stop as his mom pulled up next to him in her car, freshly showered and dressed in a new set of hospital scrubs. She smiled at her son from behind the wheel, even though the bags under her eyes still made her look tired.

"Hey, Mom," said Jim, forcing a smile in return.

"Looking sharp, Doctor Lake!" Toby said as he rolled past them, having trouble with his brakes. He stopped, eventually, and pedaled back to wave at Jim's mom.

"Thank you, Toby," said Barbara. "So are you."

"Oh?" Toby said, pleasantly surprised. He flexed his arm like a bodybuilder and sucked in his belly. "Does it show?"

Jim read the guilty look on his mom's face and knew what that meant. She was working late again.

"You're going to be out all night?" he asked.

Barbara sighed and said, "Doctor Gilberg is out with bursitis, and Doctor Lenz has a wedding out of town this weekend."

Ugh, a double shift, Jim thought. He felt so sorry for his mom. *And the food at the hospital is terrible!*

"Okay," said Jim. "Well, don't forget to bring your—"

"Dinner," Barbara said, holding up the brown paper bag with her meat loaf sandwich. "Thank you."

"Right," Jim said with a wink. "And try to find an oven to reheat it instead of nuking. It takes all the flavor away."

Jim shifted on his bike seat and felt an unexpected crinkle of paper in his front jeans pocket. Reaching inside, he fished out the sticky note with Mr. Strickler's number written across it in perfect penmanship. Jim quickly hid the paper, not wanting to burden his mom with something else on top of her nocturnal work schedule.

"Jim, there must be a million things you'd rather be doing than looking after me," said Barbara, missing her son's sleight of hand with the sticky note.

"Can't think of one," said Jim.

Barbara smiled once more at Jim before driving off and saying out the open window, "Love you, honey."

"Bye, Mom," Jim replied. Now he was the one feeling a little guilty for not telling Barbara about Mr. Strickler's concerns.

"You mother your mother a lot," said Toby.

"Ha," Jim deadpanned. "See ya tomorrow, Tobes."

The guys biked into their cul-de-sac and parted ways, Jim riding up to his home and Toby to his nana's house right across the street.

"Hey, and by the way," Toby called from his driveway, "don't use mayo on the sandwich. It's the wrong note."

Duly noted, Jim thought as he parked his bike in the garage. He then rifled through his bag for the remote to close the garage door behind him. That's when he noticed that the Amulet had been glowing bright blue. Jim looked over his shoulder, feeling as if he was being watched again, like back in the locker room.

Creeped out, he pressed the button on the clicker, and the garage door descended slowly and loudly. Just before it came all the way down, Jim glanced outside again. He could have sworn he saw something rustling in the bushes before the door blocked them from his view.

Probably raccoons, thought Jim. *Probably.*

Feeling unsettled, Jim tried to calm himself with his usual nightly ritual. He tossed his bag onto the couch and his cell onto the coffee table, and he turned on the TV. After the day he'd had, homework could wait an hour or three.

Jim retrieved the Amulet from his book bag once more and examined it carefully. It had stopped glowing, but Jim had the impression that it was still . . . active. He toggled some of its gears, but the Amulet remained inert for now.

"I am Gun Robot," said Jim's cell in a mechanical voice. "Pick up your phone."

Jim picked up his vibrating cell and answered, remembering how Toby had insisted they use this ringtone after watching their favorite sleepover movie, *Gun Robot 3*.

"Hey, Tobes," Jim said into the phone, never taking his eyes off the Amulet.

"Did it talk again?" Toby asked from the other end of the call. "Did it do anything interesting?"

Jim considered mentioning the glow and the raccoons. Maybe the Amulet was some sort of high-tech raccoon detector? But he ultimately thought better of it and settled for a simple "Nope."

"Toby-pie!" shouted Toby's nana from his end, causing Jim to move the cell a few inches away from his ear. "Dinner!"

"In a minute, Nana!" Toby shouted back, then said to Jim, "I gotta go. Text me if it does anything cool."

Jim hung up and gave up on the now-lifeless Amulet. He went back to the TV, changing channels from the news, to a commercial, to an old *Sally-Go-Back* rerun. Glancing from the screen to the Amulet, Jim discovered that it pulsed with blue light once again.

"Um . . . hi," Jim said right into the Amulet, like it was a microphone. "How are you doing? I'm Jim."

No answer from the glowing Amulet.

"But then, you knew that because you spoke my name, which is . . . weird," Jim continued. What was it about being nervous that always made him babble on like this?

"Hello?" he tried again, turning the Amulet, looking for any kind of hinge or power switch. "Anybody in there?"

Still no answer. Jim sighed.

"And now I'm talking to an inanimate object," he muttered, before squeezing the Amulet in his hand. "Come on! Talk again or you are going up on eBay!"

Jim froze when he heard a loud clatter. Not from the Amulet . . . but from the basement.

Startled, Jim set the Amulet down on the coffee table. The device's face glowed brighter than ever, not that Jim noticed. He stood up at the sound of more clattering downstairs. Only now did Jim realize just how dark it seemed inside his own house. In his rush to relax in front of the TV, he had neglected to turn on any lamps.

Jim opened the door to the basement. Another clatter sounded below.

"Raccoons," Jim said, remembering the rustling from the front bushes.

He grabbed his mom's broom and walked downstairs, more secure in the knowledge that he'd be facing off with fuzzy little critters, not . . . something else. Just as Jim reached the bottom of the steps, a dark shape backed away from the furnace, spilling a few lumps of coal.

Whoa, thought Jim. *BIG raccoon*.

Upstairs, the Amulet reacted, and its arcane gears clicked into a new configuration.

Tick.

In the basement Jim turned on an overhead

light, illuminating his surroundings. He turned a full three hundred and sixty degrees, staring into all the black, but empty, corners. Jim came all the way around and yelped in fright.

But it was just his reflection, caught in one of the old mirrors Barbara stored in the basement. Jim forced himself to calm down . . . until the light-bulb exploded behind him.

Tick.

He yelped again as the space plunged into darkness. Jim felt sweat bead around the nape of his neck, even though the basement air felt cold and thick. He stood still, unaware as six yellow eyes blinked open behind him.

Tick.

"Master Jim!" cried out Blinky in triumphant greeting.

"AAAH!" screamed Jim.

He lost his balance and fell backward onto his butt. Jim scrambled away from the six-eyed creature . . . and right into the basement's heating duct. His head whacked into the pipe with a loud thunk.

"Master Jim!" Blinky tried again.

Thunk. Jim bopped his head on the duct again.

"We have found you," Blinky continued, despite Jim's terror. "I am known as Blinky."

Jim screamed once more and crab-walked in a different direction across the basement floor, until he ran into something else. Looking up, Jim saw an even larger creature gazing down at him with a puzzled expression.

"Hi," said AAARRRGGHH!!!.

"AAAH!" Jim screamed again.

"It's 'AAARRRGGHH!!!,'" the large Troll corrected. "Three Rs."

Jim staggered to his feet, running away from AAARRRGGHH!!! and right toward Blinky's four outstretched arms. With fumbling feet, Jim avoided Blinky but accidentally bumped into the furnace and burned his hands.

Another scream.

"Hmm," mused AAARRRGGHH!!!. "He says 'AAAH!' a lot."

Jim dropped to his knees and covered his head with his arms, praying this was all just a very vivid, very messed-up dream. The two Trolls stood above him, trying to decipher the human's unusual behavior.

"It's more of a yelp, I believe," Blinky concluded. "A greeting, perhaps!"

Blinky leaned in closer and tried a scream of his own by repeating, "AAAH!"

"AAAH!" Jim screamed back, before running away.

But AAARRRGGHH!!! snagged Jim with ease and brought him back over to the warmth of the furnace. Unfortunately for Jim, the gargantuan Troll held him upside down. Jim couldn't help but think back to Toby and the gym rope, even as he covered his eyes.

"Master Jim," said Blinky. "You have been chosen."

"Blinky, he looks scared," said AAARRRGGHH!!!.

The Troll was right. Jim trembled in his grip.

"Uh, AAARRRGGHH!!!, my good fellow, would you mind?" Blinky said as he indicated the ground. "This is a moment of some solemnity."

"Solembily?" AAARRRGGHH!!! repeated.

"It means serious and dignified," explained Blinky.

AAARRRGGHH!!! tried to pronounce that last word, but the best he could manage was "Dig-oo-nified."

"P-p-put me down, please!" Jim stammered.

"Oh," said AAARRRGGHH!!!, reminded of the shivering human in his hand. He placed Jim on the basement floor, right side up, and patted him on the head.

"Thank you!" said Blinky. "Now, where was I?"

"Uh, Master Jim . . . found you . . ." AAARRRGGHH!!! said to refresh Blinky's memory.

"Yes. Thank you," said Blinky. "Master Jim, you have been chosen."

Jim didn't care. He just wanted to get out of this basement and out of this nightmare. Jim tried dodging to the left and slammed into one of AAARRRGGHH!!!'s arms. He ducked to the right and bounced off the other arm.

"The Amulet of Merlin challenges you to ascend to the most sacred of offices," Blinky said over the commotion.

"Orifices?" said AAARRRGGHH!!!, not following again. "What orifices?"

"Offices. It means responsibility," Blinky said quickly, then looked back at Jim. "Unbeknownst to your kind, there is a secret world. A vast civilization of Trolls lurking beneath your feet, hidden from view."

Jim finally stopped running in circles. "T-T-Trolls?"

"Trolls," said Blinky. "Yes, Trolls. And it is now your charge to protect them. For you, Master Jim . . . are the Trollhunter."

"Trollhunter," echoed AAARRRGGHH!!!.

"This honor is yours to accept," Blinky said while appraising Jim's terror-stricken face. "So, what say you?"

By way of answer, Jim's eyes rolled back in his head and he promptly fainted. The two Trolls looked down at the unconscious champion sprawled across the floor between them.

"Is that a yes?" asked AAARRRGGHH!!!.

CHAPTER 7
CHECKMATE

Jim kneeled alone in the basement, surrounded once again by thousands of loose parts for a Vespa scooter. Only this time, there were six headlights scattered among the hardware, not one. All six headlights blinked on and off at Jim, like three sets of otherworldly, yet familiar, eyes.

Groaning, Jim awoke with a start from the dream, still sprawled across the basement floor. The stiffness in his back told him he had been sleeping there for hours. Or maybe that was just from ping-ponging between that Troll's gigantic arms last night. They'd felt smooth, like rock, only warmer, as if there was blood pumping just under the solid surface. Jim pulled his cell from his pocket and checked the time: 7:27 a.m.

Forget texting, Jim thought. *There probably aren't emojis for giant monsters. Ones with stone . . . for skin. . . .*

As soon as he thought those last words, Jim immediately remembered how Eli had said the exact same thing from inside his locker. What was going on here?

"Pick up, pick up," said Jim as he autodialed Toby.

"Hey, Jim," answered Toby, although his mouth sounded like it was stuffed with food.

"Tobes," Jim said. "You're never gonna believe what happened last night!"

"Yeah, I'm kinda in the middle of something, Jimbo," said Toby in that odd voice again.

"I am freaking out here! Seriously freaking!" Jim said. "I need to talk to somebody."

"Chillax," said Toby. "What's going on?"

"Okay, last night I heard something in my basement," Jim began. "I thought it was raccoons, but then—"

"Yeah, hang on a second," interrupted Toby, before the shrill whine of a high-pitched drill came across the line, followed by Toby's panicked screams.

Jim nearly dropped his cell at the racket, then

realized that Toby had said he'd be at the dentist this morning. That wasn't food in Tobes's mouth. It was gauze.

"Sorry, Jim, I have to call you back," Toby managed to say, followed by more drilling.

Jim winced in sympathy and then hung up. He still felt the need to talk to someone he trusted about what happened to him last night, but who? His mom was still stuck in her double shift at the hospital.

Jim briefly entertained the idea of telling Claire. She seemed like a great listener. He would just bike to her house, reintroduce himself, and walk her through his entire encounter with two Trolls named Blinky and AAARRRGGHH!!! and . . . and . . . and who was Jim kidding? Mentioning any of this to Claire would be romantic suicide.

Looking down, Jim saw something on the basement floor: the yellow sticky note with Mr. Strickler's number. It must've fallen out of Jim's pocket when he had gone for his cell.

Jim walked as quickly as he could down the hallway at Arcadia Oaks High School, trying not to make eye contact with anybody, especially Steve. Jim didn't need any more pain this morning. Between the ache in his back and the soreness on his fingertips—Jim's chef game was so off, he'd nicked himself with the knife twice during breakfast prep—he was already hurting.

Reaching Mr. Strickler's office, Jim held his ear to the door and heard orchestra music playing from the other side. He took a deep breath and eased open the door.

"Ah, hello, Jim," said Mr. Strickler from behind his desk. "What can I do for you?"

"Um, do you have a minute?" asked Jim, his head still poking through the doorway.

"Are you all right? You look piqued," Mr. Strickler said with concern, motioning to the stool in front of his desk. "Here, sit."

Jim sat on the stool, his book bag still slung over his shoulder, and began saying, "Okay, I don't really know how to say this, but last night something incredible happened."

Mr. Strickler raised his eyebrows with curiosity. Jim suddenly realized how low the stool was compared to his teacher's seat. One of the taller students must've sat there before Jim. Feeling self-conscious, like he was a little kid at the grown-ups' table, Jim stood and spun the stool cushion on its axle to elevate it, talking as he did so.

"Actually, unbelievable. Completely unbelievable," Jim continued, distracted by the stool. "As in, you won't believe me, but I'm telling you it's true. I promise you it's true."

"All right, just calm down," Mr. Strickler said. "I'll believe you."

He took a pen from his desk and clicked it to jot down any notes, just as he often did in AP World History class. The clicking pen sound somehow reassured Jim, making him feel that this was just another normal day at school. Almost.

"Uh, okay," Jim said. "Last night two, um, things showed up at my house."

"Things?" asked Mr. Strickler, looking up from his notepad.

"You know, things," Jim said. "Guys. But really weird. One had these eyes, and the other one was huge and hairy."

Here comes the hard part, Jim thought. He inhaled and shut his eyes.

"And they said they were Tro—" Jim said, cutting off that last word.

"Tro?" Mr. Strickler repeated, looking confused.

But Jim just couldn't bring himself to say "Trolls." Sitting there, in the broad daylight that filtered into Mr. Strickler's office, Jim quickly felt foolish. Maybe it had all just been a dream, fueled by too many *Sally-Go-Back* reruns and Eli's crazy story from the day before. But Jim had to think of something else to say. He couldn't just end on "Tro."

"Tr-Trainers," Jim fibbed on the fly. "Trainers! Who want to train me in . . ."

His eyes searched Mr. Strickler's office for ideas. Jim looked past the desk, the bookcase, and the tribal masks on the wall, until he finally settled on Mr. Strickler's chess set by the window.

"Ch . . . uh . . . chess!" said Jim.

"And why would that have you so perturbed?" Mr. Strickler asked, clicking his pen.

Jim abandoned the stool, now swiveled so high up that his feet couldn't even touch the floor, and crossed to the chess set. He picked up the white knight piece with his scabbed fingers.

"They really weirded me out," Jim improvised.

He looked up from the knight and out the window. His blood ran cold. Steve Palchuk was practicing soccer on the field just outside Mr. Strickler's office. With zero effort, Steve kicked the ball, arcing it in the air so that it landed square on his teammate's head. The other guy dropped to the turf, stunned by the soccer ball. Steve then turned and found Jim watching him through Mr. Strickler's window.

"Tick-tock. Tick-tock," mouthed Steve with glee, wagging his metronome finger at Jim.

Jim felt his insides churn even as Mr. Strickler rose and joined him at the chess set.

"Now, I think I know what has you so distraught, Jim," said Mr. Strickler, taking the knight from his student.

"You do?" asked Jim, more than a little surprised.

"It's like I told you yesterday," Mr. Strickler said. "You have a lot on your shoulders. Too much, in my opinion, for someone your age. And I think this opportunity—"

"Chess?" Jim interjected, still clinging to his quickly invented lie.

"I think it's causing you anxiety," Mr. Strickler

continued. "I know you want to be there for your mother, but it's as a great poet once wrote . . ."

Mr. Strickler returned the knight to its position on the board. 6. Knight takes king. Checkmate. He toppled the king with a flick of his finger for effect.

"'Do what's good for you, or you're not good for anybody,'" said Mr. Strickler, just as the first-period bell rang in the hall.

Jim looked up from the chessboard and found his teacher smiling at him. He smiled back, feeling better.

"Hey, thanks for the advice," Jim said with all sincerity. "I like talking to you."

"Always," replied Mr. Strickler as Jim turned and left for his first class.

Walter Strickler watched Jim go, noticing the book bag across his back . . . and the Amulet peeking out from one of the unzipped pouches. Its face shone bright blue, as it had the night before.

Strickler's eyes went wide with disbelief. But there was no mistaking what he had just seen. That was the Amulet of Merlin. In Jim Lake's backpack. He was certain of it.

The teacher clicked his pen and unscrewed the

cap, revealing an unusually shaped key. Strickler removed a dictionary from his bookshelf, exposing a hidden lock. He inserted the key and accessed a secret room behind the wall.

A pair of antique battle spears from some long-lost civilization hung from the cinderblock walls. Stacks of ancient books and scrolls occupied the corners, with misshapen skulls acting as paper-weights. Strickler entered, picked up a rotary phone, and heard the call connect to the other end of the line.

"Alert the rest of the Janus Order," Strickler said into the phone, all traces of warmth gone from his voice. "After many, many years of deceit, it looks as if my patience is about to finally pay off. . . ."

CHAPTER 8
BELLY OF THE BEAST

No sooner had the sun set over Arcadia Oaks than a new activity took place in its dry canal. A small speck of intense light appeared on one of the concrete walls, then arced a semicircle about six feet in diameter. The line shattered inward, and from the magical portal of swirling rocks and light stepped Blinky and AAARRRGGHH!!!. The doorway closed behind the Trolls once they'd crossed into the surface world.

Blinky still held what looked like a crystal dagger, with more of those specks of intense light swirling within its facets. He placed the object into the pouch on his belt, licked his finger, and held it high in the air to feel the direction of the wind.

"That way," Blinky said, pointing to the woods

with his other three hands. "Bular would want to stay downwind so as to avoid detection."

The two Trolls clambered up the canal's steep incline and entered the neighboring woods. Countless broken branches and uprooted trunks let them know Bular had been this way already.

"Sure about this?" asked AAARRRGGHH!!!, his round eyes taking in the destruction.

"More or less," Blinky said, forging deeper into the woods. "After last night's . . . less than success-ful introduction, perhaps it would be wise to give Master Jim the night off, so to speak. Allow his human brain extra time to process all the informa-tion we shared."

"But hunting for Bular?" said AAARRRGGHH!!!. "We're Trolls. Not Trollhunters."

"Most certainly, my friend," Blinky agreed. "I've never been much of a fighter, nor have you these past few centuries. But if we can somehow find and capture Bular, then perhaps we needn't even bother training Master Jim."

AAARRRGGHH!!! followed Blinky deeper into the woods, periodically checking over his shoulder to make sure that no one else was following them in turn.

"But if Kanjigar couldn't . . . ," AAARRRGGHH!!! said.

"Then our chances at survival are slim to none," Blinky added, finishing the thought. "Yes, I'll admit that success seems unlikely. The best we can do is attempt to retrace the steps of Master Jim's courageous predecessor and hope we get lucky."

They reached the edge of the woods. Blinky's four arms parted some thick shrubs, revealing the abandoned Vespa factory just beyond the tree line, silent and foreboding.

"I believe the humans have a term for moments such as this," said Blinky. "Bingo."

"Bongo?" AAARRRGGHH!!! asked.

"Eh, close enough," said Blinky, before walking toward the factory, AAARRRGGHH!!! right behind him.

Wind rustled through the tall, unruly weeds growing around the factory's entrance. AAARRRGGHH!!! nudged open the rusted front door, an easy feat for a Troll his size. Blinky went in first, holding up a different crystal that glowed pale yellow, like a mystical flashlight. Their stone feet crunched on shattered glass, wads of garbage, and a downed sign that said VESPA MOTORS ASSEMBLY PLANT. Holding the crystal closer to the floor, Blinky highlighted a trail of blood drops, now dried and faded to brown.

"This is most assuredly the place," Blinky whispered.

Moving as quietly as they could, the pair rounded the next corner and gasped at the sight of the throne room. They saw the destroyed brick walls, collections of digested bones, and the large seat formed from squashed Vespa engines . . . but no Bular.

"Thank Gorgus," Blinky sighed in relief. "AAARRRGGHH!!!, we may not have much time before he returns. Let's scour the area for any clues that might prove useful in Bular's undoing."

AAARRRGGHH!!! lumbered over to the throne, sniffing at the steps beneath it. His mossy green head jerked back immediately, and he wrinkled his nose in disgust.

"Impure," AAARRRGGHH!!! said, still tasting bitterness on his tongue.

"Changelings?" Blinky asked, dropping the bent Vespa license plate he had been examining. "Here? In league with Bular? This is a dire development indeed."

Blinky moved toward the throne to smell for himself when he accidentally walked into a scrap of fabric hanging above him. Looking up, Blinky's six eyes beheld a large filthy cloth, tattered and stained. Two large metal spikes held the top corners in place high on the brick wall. Another breeze blew through the factory's empty windowpanes, fluttering the cloth and revealing something underneath.

Overcome with curiosity, Blinky tugged on the fabric, and the entire sheet came down.

"Aarghaumont," Blinky said to his friend, his mouth dry with fear. "Look!"

AAARRRGGHH!!! turned around and saw what Blinky saw. His body tensed.

A massive mural covered the factory wall, previously hidden by the cloth. Painted in faded brown with brutal brushstrokes, the chilling image depicted a large Troll with a crown of horns, clearly Bular. The painted Bular held a crude rendering of the Amulet up to a bridge. Below his hooved feet, countless drawn humans worshipped Bular from some sort of underworld. And below them an even larger painted Troll awaited, one of his eyes missing.

"Gunmar," AAARRRGGHH!!! growled, his eyes

narrowing in anger as he touched the mural.

"Gunmar the Black," Blinky repeated. "Gunmar the Vicious. Gunmar the Skullcrusher. Although Bular would simply call him 'father.'"

"What's this mean?" AAARRRGGHH!!! asked.

"Of that, I am uncertain," said Blinky.

AAARRRGGHH!!! grumbled, drawing Blinky's attention.

"AAARRRGGHH!!!?" Blinky said. "What is it?"

"Just thought of something," AAARRRGGHH!!! answered. "If Bular not here . . . then where?"

CHAPTER 9
GLORY

The blade plunged deeper, squirting red liquid everywhere. Jim's face twisted in pain as some of it splashed in his eye.

"Ow!" he said. "Stupid tomato."

Jim wiped his face with a kitchen towel and resumed slicing the tomato with his knife. He stacked the slices on the side of his Santoku and expertly deposited them on the three awaiting sandwiches. Albacore tuna salad on sourdough with scallions, wasabi mayo, and (secret ingredient) celery salt—tomorrow's lunches were done and ready to be bagged.

Wiping the blade clean, Jim spun it around his finger and flung the Santoku back into the knife block like a ninja. He'd been feeling so good since his talk with Mr. Strickler. Something about the guy's voice just put Jim at ease. He didn't even sweat it when Steve did his stupid "Tick-tock" thing again at lunch. Or when Jim spotted Claire and her friends steal a giggling look at him. It didn't matter that Toby's mouth was still numb from the novocaine, because Jim didn't need cheering up. Even that nutso dream about those two Trolls seemed like a distant memory. For once Jim was happy with his life being ordinary.

So of course the Amulet chose now to start glowing again. Jim saw the blue light shine from within his bag across the kitchen. Just like that, those carefree feelings drained out of Jim's mind.

Enough of this, Jim thought. *Strickler's right. I've got enough on my plate as it is. I'm taking that busted gizmo back to the canal and leaving it where I found it.*

Jim grabbed his bag and left through the back door. He could cut through the neighbor's yard and get to the dry canal faster than going the long way around on his bike. The wind kicked up, whispering through the trees. Jim thought he heard the Amulet's gears shift in his bag.

Tick.

Jim retrieved the Amulet and held it at an angle so he could read the back of it in the waning dusk light. All of a sudden the Amulet's outer ring began to spin like a dial and the symbols etched into it started to . . . change.

They transformed from that unfamiliar language Jim had never seen before to something that looked like Chinese or Japanese to Spanish to, finally, English. The Amulet stopped spinning, and the words "FOR THE GLORY OF MERLIN, DAYLIGHT IS MINE TO COMMAND" illuminated around its outer edge.

Jim stared at the incantation for a moment. He felt compelled to read it, just as he had felt mysteriously compelled to pull the Amulet out of that rubble the day before.

"For the glory of Merlin," said Jim, "daylight is mine to command."

And that was the exact moment Jim Lake Jr.'s life changed forever.

The wind howled harder than ever. All the animals in a four-block radius howled too, sensing the abrupt drop in pressure and a crackle of electricity in the air. By reading the incantation, Jim had triggered the Amulet in a way he'd never imagined possible.

The device shuddered before producing a small sphere of light. The brilliant orb rose into the air, trailing radiance like a comet. Floating and swirling around his head, the ball of light entranced Jim . . . before sinking into his heart. Several more orbs then issued from the Amulet and followed the first through Jim's chest.

Rather than shriek in agony, Jim felt a wave of confidence wash over him. His body lifted into the air, buoyed three feet off the lawn by the energy within him. Still hovering, Jim watched the light then explode from his body in a form similar to fireworks—fireworks that refused to obey the laws of physics. The sparks swirled and swelled, collecting around Jim's arms, legs, and torso. In what could only be an act of magic, sterling silver metal plates appeared between the arcing energy and closed around Jim's limbs as if magnetized to them.

The weight of the now-fused metal brought Jim back down to earth, and he found himself cocooned in what appeared to be a way-oversized suit of armor—too big for Jim, but just right for a

Troll. Then, as if the armor could read Jim's mind, it contracted, shrinking down to his smaller proportions. The resizing sent more of that electric blue light coursing along the engravings in the armor. The zigzagging lines of energy all converged over Jim's heart, where the Amulet now rested, embedded in the armored breastplate.

Jim looked down at his transformed body, curling his fingers inside their new gauntlets. It all felt so real against his skin. This wasn't a prank. This wasn't a dream. This was happening. As this realization rushed into Jim's mind, he felt like he should say something special—something important—to commemorate this occasion.

"This is so cool!" Jim shouted in joy. Well, that would have to do for now.

He struck a pose, standing akimbo like a superhero, feeling the armor glide smoothly with his every movement. But the Amulet wasn't done yet.

Five more spheres of light sprang from its inner workings and coalesced in Jim's right hand. A shock wave of energy expanded outward from his palm, and a marvelously large sword manifested out of thin air. Jim tried holding its hilt with two hands, but the heft of the shimmering blade brought it down to the ground. The Daylight sword was simply too heavy for Jim to lift. Jim sighed with disappointment.

But as with the armor, the weapon reduced and conformed to Jim's measurements. He raised Daylight again, ethereal mist cascading off its razor-sharp edges. Now, this was a blade Jim could handle!

Drawing upon his vast kitchen knife skills—and all the cool swordplay moves he and Tobes had seen in *Gun Robot* parts 1 through 4—Jim swung Daylight across the darkening night air. He heard its keen edges shear through the atmosphere, tasted the residual energy still glimmering around its bejeweled guard, felt the balance of the blade in his hand.

This, thought Jim. *This is that "something more" I've always wanted.*

He wielded Daylight like a warrior, slicing and slashing. Preparing for a truly mighty strike, Jim brought the sword far behind his back . . . and accidentally sank it into one of the boulders decorating his backyard.

He tugged at Daylight. It didn't budge.

Jim tried two hands. No luck.

He stood on the boulder and pulled with his entire body, trying to gain leverage. And it worked! Only for the sword to then sink into another boulder behind him.

"Aw, come on!" Jim yelled.

As he pulled on Daylight, Jim thought of the old stories about the Sword in the Stone that his mom used to read to him as a boy. Didn't King Arthur have a wizard friend? Wasn't his name Merlin? Could that Merlin and the one written on the Amulet be the same?

Less than a mile away Walter Strickler walked the length of the dry canal, his loafers echoing along its drab gray walls. He stopped at what was left of Kanjigar's remains, now scattered across the canal as if kicked aside by a petulant child. Strickler knew Bular was behind him before he even smelled the evil Troll's rancid breath.

"It's been taken," Strickler said. "You failed. You let it go. Your father will be displeased."

Bular roared into Strickler's ear, his eyes burning

in the night like two hot coals. He had spent the last day and night searching Arcadia Oaks for the Amulet, clinging to the shadows and stopping only long enough to snack on the humans unfortunate enough to spot him. The last thing the son of Gunmar needed right now was a lecture from this Impure.

"Whoever holds the Amulet of Merlin," growled Bular, "I shall destroy him, just as I have done with every single one of them."

"Worry not, you brute." Strickler smirked. "I know where to find it."

Strickler's eyes then shone in the night as brightly as Bular's.

"I believe the Amulet has found its champion," he added, his pupils as red as blood.

CHAPTER 10
THE SWORD IN THE STONE

Once Jim had finally freed Daylight from the second stone, he spent the rest of the night testing out his new weapon and armor. When his arms got tired from swinging and chopping at the air, he found that he could magnetically affix the sword onto his back. It didn't take too long for Jim to feel energized again and go back to his practice with a smile. He kept going like this beyond midnight and into the early morning, stopping only when the sun came up. Jim hadn't slept a wink all night, but it didn't matter. He'd never felt so awake in his whole life.

Of course, Jim couldn't cook or attend school in this armor, so he struggled a bit with how to remove it. Piece by piece? Was there an enchanted zipper somewhere? He took out the Amulet and studied it. On an impulse he turned the dial, and he was immediately back in his own clothes. It was incredible. Jim simply had to share this with someone. And he knew just the guy. . . .

After cooking and bagging three medianoche sandwiches in record time, Jim paid a visit to the dentist's office before heading to school.

"Don't go in there," warned Gloria, the dental assistant. "He's with a patient."

But for Jim, news like this couldn't wait. He opened the door to the procedure room and, sure enough, found Toby about to undergo day two of his orthodontic "tune-up."

"Tobes," said Jim breathlessly.

"Hey, Jim," Toby replied, but it came out a little garbled with the dentist's finger stuck in his mouth.

"Tobes! Tobes, Tobes, Tobes, Tobes!" Jim repeated. "I have got to talk to you!"

"Uh, Imma ittle uthy ight ow," said Toby from his reclined position in the dentist's chair.

"What?" Jim asked.

"He says he's a little busy right now," said Doctor Muelas, translating for his patient, before jamming some spacers between Toby's molars.

"Oh God, it hurts," Toby groaned.

That, Jim understood. But he pressed on, saying, "Okay, remember that thing we found the other day? In the canal. The thing with the gem and stuff? It works! It works like crazy!"

"Is ant ate an?" Toby gurgled.

"What?" Jim asked again.

"He says, 'This can't wait, man?'" translated Doctor Muelas.

"I've already waited until morning," said Jim. "Who goes to the dentist two days in a row?"

Toby said a few more words, but the whir of the dentist's drill drowned them out.

"'I want to get these braces off before I'm thirty,'" Doctor Muelas translated once again. "'It's like my mouth is a city engineering project.'"

"How much longer is this going to take?" Jim asked.

Eight hours later the two returned to Jim's house. And for once Jim actually wanted the distraction of classes, even if it meant risking a run-in with Steve. Anything would have been better than sitting in a dentist's waiting room all day with a secret this big.

"Okay, Tobes," Jim began. "You are never going to believe this."

"My mouth still feels a little sore," Toby said, rubbing his jaw.

As Toby searched the refrigerator for something cold to hold against his teeth, Jim grabbed the Amulet from his bag.

"Check this out," said Jim, getting ready to read the incantation, when . . .

"Do you have any aspirin?" Toby asked, killing the mood.

"Tobes, pay attention," Jim sighed.

But that would be impossible for Toby. He had found a box of frozen pizza. The aroma of pepperoni and mushrooms made Toby forget about his pain and whatever Jim was up to.

"For the glory of Merlin," Jim read from the Amulet. "Daylight is mine to co—"

A kitchen timer went off, interrupting Jim once more. He looked from the Amulet to Toby, who pulled the cooked pizza from the microwave.

"Go on," Toby said, before taking a bite.

"It worked last night," Jim said, not getting it.

He had read the magic words, so where was the armor? Maybe all of Toby's distractions were annoying the Amulet as much as Jim? Taking a deep breath, Jim cleared his mind and relaxed his body. As if on cue, the Amulet floated out of his hand and expelled fresh bolts of energy. Other objects around the kitchen also began to levitate— including Toby's slice of pizza.

"Holy champignon!" Toby exclaimed.

Toby watched his best friend rise into the air. In a flash, the suit of armor formed around Jim's body, fitting like a glove. Daylight remained on Jim's back as he had left it at sunrise.

"How cool is that?" said Jim, still amazed by the transformation.

"Whaaaaaaaaaat?" gasped Toby in disbelief. "Oh my gosh! Oh my gosh! Oh my gosh! Oh my gosh!"

Tobes ran over to Jim and touched his armor. Its surface still tingled with magic. It felt a little electric, like being shocked when you shook someone's hand.

"So cool! So cool! So cool!" he kept repeating. "Dude, you know what this means, right? You have a sacred responsibility here."

"That's what they said!" blurted Jim.

"You have to use these new powers for the benefit of all mankind," said Toby between bites of pizza. "You have to use this to kick Steve's butt."

Jim's jaw dropped in disappointment.

"Really?" Jim said, shaking his head. "I show you a glowing sword and a suit of armor that can only be magic, and that's how you respond?"

"Seriously! It's butt-kicking time," Toby said, before launching into some made-up karate moves. Around the fifth jump kick, he paused.

"Wait," said Toby. "Who's 'they'?"

The back door promptly swung open, and in walked Blinky with a friendly laugh.

"Master Jim!" said the Troll, trying his hardest to sound upbeat. After what he had seen in Bular's lair last night—and Jim's fainting spell the night before—Blinky knew this would be a tricky conversation. Especially once Jim's friend started screaming.

"What—what—what is that?" Toby stammered. "I'm calling 911!"

AAARRRGGHH!!!'s head then leaned into the open doorway, making Toby scream again.

"No, Animal Control!" Toby decided as he ducked behind the kitchen island and started dialing on his cell.

AAARRRGGHH!!! shoved his way inside Jim's house, his powerfully wide shoulders splintering the doorjamb on the way through. He looked at Blinky.

"Door small," AAARRRGGHH!!! said with a sheepish smile.

"Monsters at my best friend's house!" Toby shouted into his cell. "I need you to send a squad! Make that the National Guard!"

Jim and the Trolls watched as Toby lowered his phone in defeat and said, "Animal Control hung up on me."

"You told your friend about us?" Blinky asked Jim.

"Um, is that a problem?" said Jim.

"Master Jim, we Trolls have gone to great lengths to keep our existence secret from your kind, lest there be panic," Blinky explained.

AAARRRGGHH!!! peeked behind the kitchen island, surprising Toby. The Troll gently picked up the boy and inspected him like a new toy, poking his belly. Toby screamed again.

"Like that," Blinky added.

AAARRRGGHH!!! lowered Toby onto the counter. Rifling through the kitchen drawers, Toby grabbed a soup ladle and swung it around like a hammer to shoo away the Troll.

"This is my best friend, Toby D.," said Jim to Blinky and AAARRRGGHH!!!.

Blinky smiled warmly, dodging the ladle and telling Toby, "Your friend is the Trollhunter. His noble obligation is protective."

"You mean, like a superhero?" Toby asked, lowering the ladle. "Oh, can I be his sidekick? With a cool superhero name like Deathblade or Snipersnake?"

"Just wait," said Jim. "Who would I be protecting?"

"Us," grumbled AAARRRGGHH!!!.

"And mankind," Blinky added. "From bad Trolls. As well as Goblins, Gruesomes, and the occasional rogue Gnome. The mantle of Trollhunter is a sacred responsibility. One which has never been passed to a human before. This is a momentous occasion."

Just as Blinky's words sank in, Jim jolted at a horn honking. He peeked out the window and saw his mom's car pull into the driveway.

"Oh, it's my mother!" Jim exclaimed.

How was Jim going to explain to her why he was wearing armor and chatting with two Trolls instead of doing his homework?

CHAPTER 11
FLUSHED AWAY

"Upstairs! Quick!" ordered Jim, hurrying Toby, Blinky, and AAARRRGGHH!!! up the staircase to the second floor.

AAARRRGGHH!!!'s incredibly strong backside accidentally knocked the banister off-kilter. But he was able to move it back into place and stomp upstairs before Barbara opened the front door.

"Jim, it's me," she said, hearing a very loud thud come from upstairs.

Jim, Toby, and the Trolls all huddled nervously in the bathroom. With so many bodies crowded among the sink, tub, and toilet, it was a pretty tight fit. Jim wriggled, trying to get more comfortable.

"She's not supposed to be home until midnight!" said Jim in an agitated whisper.

Toby was pressed against AAARRRGGHH!!!. The large Troll sniffed Toby's hair and sighed in delight.

"Mmm. You smell like cat," said AAARRRGGHH!!!, a little too loud for Jim's liking.

"My nana has a Siamese," said Toby.

"Tasty," AAARRRGGHH!!! replied, licking his lips.

The group flinched when they heard Barbara speak from the other side of the bathroom door. Jim tried turning the lock, then remembered that it had been broken for weeks.

"I forgot my phone," said Barbara. "Are you okay in there?"

"Um, fine," Jim lied, his mind grasping for excuses. "I mean, my stomach's a little, uh . . ."

Toby jammed the toilet brush in and out of the commode, making all kinds of disgusting sloshing sounds. Mortified, Jim shot his best friend a dirty look. *Dude? Seriously?!* Toby gave Jim an enthusiastic thumbs-up. Problem solved.

"Uh, you know, I might have a food poisoning situation . . . ," Jim groaned.

Taken aback by the wet gurgling noises still coming from the bathroom, Barbara said, "Honey, I'll get you some medicine, okay?"

Barbara went downstairs, and Jim gritted his teeth. This was the last thing he wanted. There was no way he was going to open the door, even a crack, and risk his mom seeing the armor. Or the Trolls. The Amulet began flashing erratically.

Jim pointed at the device in alarm and whispered to Blinky, "Okay, what's going on here?"

"The Amulet reacts to your emotional state," said Blinky. "You appear to be in some distress."

"You think?" Jim asked sarcastically.

Toby finally eased up on the toilet brush, in deep concentration, his brow furrowed. "If Jim's the first human Trollhunter, like you said, then who or what was the Trollhunter before him?" he asked the Trolls.

"The glorious mantle has been passed from Troll to Troll for hundreds of years," said Blinky.

"So, the previous Trollhunter, what, retired?" Jim asked.

"Was felled," AAARRRGGHH!!! said, lowering his head in sadness.

"Turned to stone and smashed," Blinky clarified. "Kanjigar the Courageous was his name. Brutally slain by a ruthless Troll named Bular."

Jim suddenly felt dizzy. He leaned against the door, longing for the days when a beating from Steve seemed like the worst that could happen to him. Toby caught his friend freaking out and patted him on his armor.

"Don't worry, dude," Toby said. "This Bular guy probably just got lucky."

"The evidence does not suggest that," said Blinky. "Bular is a formidable opponent."

The Amulet flashed faster, mirroring Jim's distress.

"Then the other guy . . . ," Jim said. "He was just off his game or something . . . right?"

"Doubtful. Kanjigar was perhaps the most alert and able of all the Trollhunters," Blinky said.

"But not the best, I'm betting," said Jim, a bit of hope still left in his voice.

"Oh, the very best," Blinky replied, unaware of the color draining from Jim's face. "Many songs and sagas have been written about him."

Toby stepped in and said, "Uh, I think what my friend here is a little worried about is, if Bular could defeat Kanjigar, then what's going to happen to Jim?"

"A most appropriate, if troubling, query, Tobias," said Blinky. "Of course, we would never expect Master Jim to engage in battle without the proper training."

"See? Nothing to worry about," Toby smiled, trying to cheer Jim up. "How long does the training normally take?"

Blinky started counting the fingers on his four hands. Behind him, AAARRRGGHH!!! enjoyed all the features a human bathroom has to offer. He turned the lights on and off, stuck the toilet brush in his ear, and chewed on hand soaps.

"Oh . . . decades," Blinky estimated.

"And how long do I have?" Jim asked, not really wanting to hear the answer.

"A day or two," Blinky said with an apologetic grimace.

Jim felt as if the floor had dropped out from under him . . . until Barbara knocked once again at the bathroom door.

"Jim, I have medicine and ginger ale," she said. "Come on out."

Jim held the doorknob in place so that it wouldn't turn. Toby and the Trolls scrambled backward, away from the door. The Amulet flashed like crazy, nearly blinding Jim.

"I'm fine!" he said. "Really! I just need a little privacy."

"You're worrying me," said Barbara. "I'm coming in."

Thinking fast, Jim flushed the toilet and turned the Amulet just as Barbara turned the doorknob. She opened the door, and Jim walked out in his normal clothes.

"See? All good," Jim said with an innocent look on his face.

Barbara held her nose, looked into the bathroom, and found it empty. Shrugging, she followed Jim downstairs. A few seconds later Toby, Blinky, and AAARRRGGHH!!! peered out from their cramped hiding place behind the shower curtain. AAARRRGGHH!!! took another deep whiff of Toby's hair.

"Stop sniffing me, giant Troll dude!" Toby whispered.

"Smell like cat," AAARRRGGHH!!! sighed back.

As soon as Barbara found her phone, hugged Jim good-bye, and drove away, Toby and the Trolls crept downstairs. They joined Jim in the living room, where he appeared lost in thought. He only snapped out of it when AAARRRGGHH!!!'s large body crashed into the ceiling light and knocked a bunch of books and old VHS tapes from the shelf.

"Your cave too small," AAARRRGGHH!!! decided.

"So, Master Jim, are you ready?" asked Blinky. "We should begin your training immediately."

"Uh, it's a school night," said Jim, still on edge. "I can't be out, y'know, Trollhunting. Besides, the whole 'getting killed by a vicious Troll named Bular' thing might be a deal breaker!"

"'Deal breaker'?" said Blinky, having never heard this human term before.

Jim looked around the living room for something normal, something to remind him of how his life used to be just two days ago. Instead, he saw Toby feeding AAARRRGGHH!!!.

"Dude, he eats VHS tapes!" Toby exclaimed.

AAARRRGGHH!!! belched in satisfaction, and Jim snapped.

"I don't want to die!" Jim yelled.

He didn't care so much about his own fate. It was his mom's. Who would take care of her if Jim wasn't around? He removed the Amulet from his back pocket and offered it to Blinky.

"Maybe you should take this back," said Jim.

Blinky closed his four hands around the Amulet and pushed it back toward Jim.

"The Amulet called to you, Master Jim," Blinky said. "It chose you. It is your—"

"Please don't say 'destiny,'" interrupted Jim.

"—sacred obligation," continued Blinky, even though he was totally going to say "destiny."

Jim put the Amulet back in his pocket and shook his head in dismay.

"You cannot refuse it," said Blinky. "You cannot give it back. It is yours until you die."

"And I would like to get a little further past puberty before that happens," Jim said.

"Master Jim, you are now responsible for the protection of two worlds, human and Troll alike," Blinky began anew. "If you do not keep the balance, evil Trolls like Bular will come into yours and wreak havoc."

Jim was about to argue again with Blinky, but his next words caught in his throat. Instead, he actually considered what the Troll had just said. Blinky smiled, confident that he was starting to make some progress in convincing his new Trollhunter.

"You're saying this Bular could . . . hurt people?" asked Jim.

"Like you," said AAARRRGGHH!!! between bites of VHS.

And just like that, Jim went pale again. Blinky shot AAARRRGGHH!!! a dirty look with all six of his eyes.

"Not! Helping!" Blinky said. He faced Jim once more and explained, "With the Amulet in your possession, Bular will seek you out, and you will face him, one way or another."

Toby knew that panicked look on Jim's face all too well. He stood at his friend's side and started negotiating with Blinky.

"Maybe what Jim needs is a little time to process all of this," said Toby. "You laid a lot of heavy stuff on him tonight."

Blinky considered it, feeling a twinge of sympathy for Jim. Becoming the Trollhunter was an overwhelming responsibility for even the toughest of Trolls. He could only imagine how the responsibility might affect a far more inferior creature such as a human.

"Fine, fine," said Blinky. "We shall return tomorrow, then, to begin your training."

"Awesomesauce," said Toby, sealing the deal.

He held open the back door for the Trolls to leave Jim's house discreetly. As AAARRRGGHH!!! downed a few videos for the road, Blinky looked back and saw Jim standing by himself. He appeared lost, frightened, and so very young.

"Master Jim, if I may," said Blinky in a soft voice. "Destiny is a gift."

Jim faced the Troll, his eyes wide and searching.

"Some go their entire lives living existences of quiet desperation, never learning the truth," Blinky continued. "That what feels as though a burden pushing down upon our shoulders is actually a sense of purpose that lifts us to greater heights."

Jim pulled out the Amulet again and considered it. So many emotions—fear, excitement, joy, anger, confusion—swirled in his head.

"Never forget that fear is but the precursor to valor," added Blinky. "That to strive and triumph in the face of fear is what it means to be a hero."

Hero. The word made Jim think back to the night before, when he'd unlocked the armor. Swinging that sword in the air, he felt different. Proud. Special.

"Don't think, Master Jim," said Blinky. "Become."

With that, Blinky bowed his head and departed with AAARRRGGHH!!!, Toby went home, and Jim was left alone with his thoughts.

CHAPTER 12
TWENTY-FOUR HOURS TO LIVE

Don't think. Become.

Blinky's words haunted Jim even as he pedaled his bike down the block. Jim felt the cool night air against his skin and sweat beading under his helmet. He didn't really know where he was going. But if this was going to be his last night of freedom—or life—then Jim didn't want to spend it cooped up in his house. Once Toby went back to his nana's for dinner, Jim just hopped on his bike and left.

Jim had so much on his mind, he couldn't even think of recipes for tomorrow's meals. It didn't matter if this Bular was out there somewhere, just waiting to add Jim to his long list of slain Trollhunters. Jim needed to get away, clear his mind, and pretend he was an average fifteen-year-old again.

He must've biked for a solid hour before stopping to take a break on a sidewalk. Jim unfastened his helmet, shook out his hair, and looked around the pleasant neighborhood. All around him, families sat down together for dinner, parents helped kids with homework, and teens texted and gamed with one another.

But not Jim. That kind of normal life clearly wasn't meant for him.

Jim sighed and rolled his eyes. That's when he noticed the signs staked into the lawn in front of him. They all read VOTE NUÑEZ. Jim's eyes went wide. He looked past the lawn into the house and saw Claire through the living room window.

Jim's heart skipped. He was standing in front of Claire Nuñez's house. Alone. At night. How had he wound up here, of all places? Had his mind, so clouded with Blinky's warnings, subconsciously led him here?

He watched Claire reach into a playpen and lift up her baby brother, Enrique. Jim had overheard Claire showing pictures of him on her phone to Mary and Darci.

They look so happy, Jim thought as Claire raised

Enrique higher and buried her nose into his belly. The baby giggled, and Claire laughed too.

A new thought soon followed. *Blinky said Bular might hurt people in our world*, Jim remembered. *People like Claire. And Enrique. Even Toby and Mom.*

Jim regarded the Amulet in his hand. He felt the weight of it on his palm, but also its power.

If I have the chance to help them—and others like them—shouldn't I take it?

Jim looked back at Claire's house, as if hoping to find his answer there. Instead, he found Claire standing at the window, holding Enrique in her arms and squinting in Jim's direction.

"Gah!" Jim cried, before awkwardly covering his face with his helmet and biking away in a weird, wobbly spectacle.

Jim left in such a hurry, he failed to notice the two beings that had been spying on him. Walter Strickler stepped out of the shadows across the street, followed by the snarling Bular.

"I should have devoured him on this very spot," said Bular, "and excreted the Amulet in the morning."

"Charming as ever, Bular," Strickler said in disgust. "But that would be an extremely foolish move, even for you."

Bular reached for his swords, but Strickler turned around and held the dark Troll's arms in place with surprising strength. Only this wasn't the normal Walter Strickler.

In a flash, he transformed into his true form—the tall, gaunt Changeling who had kneeled before Bular in the abandoned factory. The glow from his yellow eyes illuminated Strickler's scaly green skin and the gray horns protruding from his skull.

"Stay your hands, Son of Gunmar," hissed Strickler. The metal blades worn around his neck clinked together as he spoke. "Since most humans don't know Trolls exist, they'll never notice if a failure like Kanjigar disappears. But if a human teenager suddenly vanishes without a trace . . ."

Strickler pointed his talon at a nearby street lamp with a flyer taped to its post. "HAVE YOU SEEN THIS PERSON?" read the headline just above a picture of a missing park ranger from the woods. Bular vaguely remembered how he had tasted.

"That kind of attention could disrupt our entire

plan with Merlin's Amulet and the bridge," Strickler said. "And you wouldn't want to disappoint Daddy, now, would you?"

Bular eyed Strickler with pure hatred. He released his swords back into their scabbards and spat black phlegm onto the sidewalk.

"So be it, Impure," growled Bular. "We'll play your Changeling games . . . for now."

CHAPTER 13
OPEN MIC KNIGHT

"So, what did you decide?" Toby asked Jim as they parked their bikes and entered their school's breezeway. Toby had been dying to ask, but Jim spent most of the ride to Arcadia Oaks High School in distracted silence.

"That if anyone finds out what happened in my kitchen last night, we'll both be committed," Jim said half-jokingly.

"I meant about kicking Steve's butt!" said Toby, karate chopping the air in front of him.

"Give up the dream, Tobes," Jim sighed, just before the Amulet chimed in his book bag.

Tick.

Toby peeked into Jim's bag, which was lit up from within by the glowing Amulet, and asked,

"Does this thing run on batteries? What's it doing?"

"How should I know?" said Jim, shooing Toby away from his bag. "It didn't come with a manual!"

"Does it feel like you're gonna, y'know, change?" said Toby.

"Oh no . . . ," muttered Jim, getting a mental picture of the entire student body laughing at him in his suit of armor.

"We gotta get you someplace that's not out here!" Toby said.

He hurried Jim out of the breezeway and through the door to the locker room, drawing only a few stares—including one from Strickler, who had watched their entire exchange from afar in his human form.

Strickler opened the locker room door and followed the boys. He heard a loud metal clanging sound, followed by their hushed voices.

"Jim?" Strickler called out. "Jim, are you in here?"

The Changeling in disguise turned the corner and found Toby blocking his path.

"Oh!" Toby said with a nervous smile. "Hey, Mr. Strickler!"

"Ah, Toby," said Strickler, playing dumb. "Have you seen Jim? I believe he came in here."

"Yeah, he, um . . . he's having some issues, y'know? Taco Tuesday. Vicious!" said Toby.

On the other side of the lockers, Jim, now clad in his armor, rolled his eyes.

Again with the upset stomach? Jim thought. *Why does Tobes keep using that excuse?! And what's up with this armor? I didn't even say the incantation! It just assembled around me like it was trying to . . . I don't know, protect me from something. But what?*

Strickler sidestepped Toby and discovered Jim standing in the armor of the Trollhunter. The Changeling commanded every muscle in his face to not betray his surprise—or how he recognized that suit from when Kanjigar had worn it.

"Jim," Strickler said, forcing his voice to be calm, "I don't believe that's appropriate school attire. Do you?"

"Oh, yeah, this," Jim started rambling. "Funny story about this. It's, uh . . ."

Jim's eyes scanned the locker room for something—anything—that might help, just as he had done in Strickler's office the other day. One of Claire's *Romeo and Juliet* posters hung on the bulletin board behind Strickler.

"For *Romeo and Juliet*!" Jim said.

"Yeah, it's for the tryouts!" Toby added.

"Yes! The tryouts for *Romeo and Juliet*," said Jim.

"Jim's gonna totally smoke those auditions," Toby said as he tapped on Jim's armor. "I mean, look at his costume. It's so realistic!"

Strickler's eyes narrowed. He knew the boys were lying to him, but he suspected there might be an advantage to keeping this charade going. For a little longer, at least.

"What about chess club?" he asked.

"Oh, uh . . . I'm doing that, too, apparently," stammered Jim.

"Well, you'd better hurry, then," Strickler said with a sly grin. "I believe auditions end in five minutes."

Jim bit his lip, realizing the mental picture he'd just had about the entire student body laughing at him in his suit of armor was about to come true. . . .

Mr. Strickler personally escorted Jim and Toby to the school auditorium's backstage area. None of them said a word as they went, but Jim couldn't shake the feeling that his teacher was . . . grading him until the very moment he left them.

Jim's concerns melted, though, when he watched Claire read her lines onstage. She was so natural up there, just like when she'd jammed out to Papa Skull at her mother's fund-raiser. Every line Claire recited sounded so honest, so true.

Ms. Janeth, the play director/math teacher, clapped along with a few other drama students. Claire smiled and went to the wings, where Jim and Toby tried to hide behind the stage curtains. She was about to ask Jim what he was doing outside of her house last night, when she noticed his suit of armor.

"And here I thought you didn't like Shakespeare," Claire said to Jim.

"Oh, no, he's my favorite," Jim answered. "I totally love him."

"That costume is incredible," said Claire, eyeing the armor and the Daylight sword on Jim's back. "Did you make it?"

"No, he found a magical Amulet that makes it," Toby blurted out.

"You're funny," Claire said with the sweetest laugh Jim had ever heard.

"Yeah, you're a real comedian, aren't you?" muttered Jim between clenched teeth.

"Next," called Ms. Janeth from the audience.

Claire stepped aside, gestured to the stage, and said, "I think that's your cue."

Jim swallowed hard. Is this what it had come to? Humiliating himself just to cover up some secret destiny that he didn't even want in the first place?

"Break a leg," Claire said.

"I'd prefer that," said Jim as he took the stage.

The drama kids gaped at Jim's gleaming armor. In the front row Eli Pepperjack looked down at his own homemade cardboard costume and suddenly felt very underdressed.

"Who are you?" asked Ms. Janeth.

Jim wondered why his math teacher didn't recognize him, especially since he sat at the front of her class. Then he remembered her terrible eyesight and how crazy he must look in his armor right now.

"James Lake Jr.," Jim said in a small voice.

"And what are you trying out for?" said Ms. Janeth.

Jim guessed it didn't really matter, since he didn't know the first thing about this play anyway. But then he figured that if Claire was going to get the part of Juliet (and how couldn't she after that amazing audition?), then being Romeo might lead to more time with her on—and off—the stage. Provided he didn't die from embarrassment or a Troll mauling before that.

"Uh, Romeo," Jim said.

"Well, we are all ears," said Ms. Janeth.

The auditorium fell into silence, although Jim heard a few drama students whisper about his armor. To drown out their comments, he just started talking.

"Uh, destiny," Jim began.

He looked to the side of the stage, expecting Claire to be texting on her phone or rolling her eyes. But Claire was smiling at Jim, her eyes full of encouragement.

"Destiny is a gift," Jim continued, energized by Claire's smile.

The Amulet shone brighter on his chest, and Blinky's words flowed through Jim's mind as clearly as they had the night before.

"Some go their entire lives living existences of quiet desperation, never learning the truth," he said, his voice building. "That what feels as though a burden pushing down upon our shoulders is actually the sense of purpose that lifts us to greater heights."

Jim removed Daylight from his back and held it high in the air. The audience gasped as the stage lights reflected off the shimmering sword.

"Never forget that fear is but the precursor to valor," Jim went on, his words carrying across the entire auditorium. "That to strive and triumph in the face of fear is what it means to be a hero."

Claire worked her way from backstage to a front seat in the crowd, never taking her eyes from Jim. He looked so confident up there, yet still reminded Claire of the nice boy who'd danced with his mom at that party.

"Don't think," said Jim.

He twirled Daylight through the air and returned it to his back with a flourish.

"Become."

The audience detonated with cheers, giving Jim a standing ovation. Toby beamed from the wings, while Strickler glowered from a recessed corner.

Claire approached the stage, and Jim kneeled before her like her knight in shining armor.

"Jim, that was remarkable," said Claire.

"Really?" Jim asked. "I didn't even think. I just sort of said it."

Claire laughed, touched his armored arm, and said, "That's acting!"

Jim knew two things to be true in that very moment. One, he would never polish the part of the armor that Claire had just touched. He wanted to see her perfect fingerprints there until the day he died. Which was probably going to be today. And two, this felt like much more than acting to Jim. This felt like the freedom he experienced when he let go of his bike's handlebars or he'd summoned his armor for the first time.

By getting out of his own head for a change, Jim stopped thinking and became the guy he'd always wanted to be.

CHAPTER 14
WATCH FOR FALLING TRUCKS

"Dude! That was amazing!" said Toby to Jim as they biked home. "You were amazing! I'm amazed at how amazing you were!"

"I can't believe that just happened," Jim replied.

Everything after his audition seemed like a dream to Jim now. Waving good-bye to Claire as her dad picked her up from school, privately removing the armor in a men's room stall, even pedaling down quiet Main Street with Toby was just one big blur. Jim could not have been happier.

If only he knew that Bular stalked him from one block away. The evil Troll kept to the elongated shadows made by the setting sun. Prowling the alleys behind Arcadia Oaks's storefronts, Bular kept his burning eyes on the human child. He didn't care what Strickler said. The son of Gunmar had endured enough waiting—centuries of it, in fact. He wanted that Amulet. And he wanted it now.

Bular watched "the Trollhunter" and his tasty-looking friend turn and take a shortcut through an empty construction zone. This was his time to strike. Bular could feel it in his horns. He stepped onto the shadowed street, his heavy footfalls alerting the two small humans to Bular's arrival. He sneered at the fear in their bulging eyes.

"Trollhunter," Bular announced. "Merlin's creation. Gunmar's bane."

Jim and Toby braked hard at the sight of the biggest, ugliest Troll they had ever seen. This had to be Bular. They looked around for help, but Main Street was empty, all its shops closed for the day.

"I think he's talking to you," Toby muttered.

Bular roared and pounded the pavement with his fists. This was his typical war dance before fighting an enemy to the death. He took a swipe in Jim's direction, only to pull back his sizzling hand in pain.

A thin ray of sunlight separated Bular from the humans. And it grew thinner by the second as the sun set behind them. Bular watched the sunlight anxiously.

"Look!" said Jim. "He's afraid of the sun!"

Toby noticed how dark the sky was getting and said, "Not for long!"

"The Amulet," snarled Bular. "Surrender it and I will give you a speedy death."

Jim and Toby turned their bikes around and took off in the opposite direction.

"Doesn't know how to negotiate, this guy!" said Toby. "Go! Go! Go!"

Bular barreled down a parallel street and followed them. Getting ahead of the humans, Bular cut them off at the end of the block . . . only to find the street empty. His prey had somehow evaded him. With the sun now fully set, Bular marched down the block, hunting for the Trollhunter.

A few car lengths ahead of Bular, Jim and Toby ducked between two large construction trucks, trying to get the Amulet to work.

"Armor up, armor up, armor up!" Toby whispered in a frenzy. "Please, now! Faster!"

Jim tried clearing his mind and concentrating. But that was kind of tough, with Bular half a block away, smashing everything in his path.

"Okay," Jim whispered. "For the glory of Merlin, Daylight is mine to command."

He closed his eyes, awaiting the feel of the armor around his body. Nothing happened.

"It's not working!" Jim said in alarm.

Bular lurched closer. He could smell the boys' terror in the air.

"For the glory of Merlin, Daylight is mine to command!" Jim tried again, to no effect. "Seriously! It's mine to command. I'm commanding here!"

The truck behind Jim and Toby suddenly groaned and rose ten feet in the air. Bular held it there. He glared down upon them like they were two bugs hiding under a rock.

"Centuries of Trollhunters," Bular said, "and I will have killed two in almost as many days."

The humans uttered something in fear, but their pathetic language did not matter to Bular. Only the Amulet—and how it could restore his long-lost father to power—mattered to the son of Gunmar. He hurled the truck at the two fleeing boys.

Pumping his legs as fast as he could, Jim looked

over his shoulder. He saw the truck plummeting toward them and cried, "Flying truck!"

"Incoming!" Toby shouted.

He and Jim turned their bikes hard at a corner, narrowly missing the crash. Toby screamed when another truck landed a few feet away.

Bular now pursued them, running on all fours like a bloodthirsty gorilla. He ducked into an open construction trench on the sidewalk, disappearing underground.

"I think we lost him!" said Toby when he saw the coast was clear.

"Oh, right, because my luck has been great this week!" said Jim in full-on sarcasm mode.

Directly below them Bular bounded along in the sewers, splashing through foul water and waste. He looked up and tracked Jim and Toby's shadows through the slits in the storm drains. Bular jumped and punched the sewer ceiling.

The impact sent a manhole cover rocketing up directly in front of Jim, nearly cutting him in two.

"See?" cried Jim.

"Maybe it was just an exploding pocket of sewer gas!" guessed Toby, trying to sound hopeful. "Or it could have been someone's pet alligator! Those things get flushed down the toilet all the time as babies, then grow into—"

Another manhole cover shot into the sky, whizzing right past Toby's head.

"You know what? You're right," Toby whimpered. "Your luck sucks."

Bular burst through another open trench, flattening barricades and overturning an unmanned bulldozer.

"I'll flay the flesh from your bones!" Bular promised.

"I like my bones the way they are, thanks!" said Toby.

Bular leaped in the air and came thundering down directly in front of them, still reeking of the sewer. Jim and Toby swerved on their bikes, barely avoiding his slashing claws. His heart racing, Jim looked around the block, recognizing it.

"Head down Delancy," he said to Toby. "Behind Stuart Electronics!"

They rode faster, faster, but Bular still gained on them, tearing up the road with his hooves as he ran, snarling at Jim and Toby all the way.

"You know I can't fit there!" Toby said.

"You can fit!" Jim yelled, remembering how he and little Toby used to play behind the electronics store as kids while their families shopped inside.

With Bular right behind them, Jim turned and shot down the narrow alley behind Stuart Electronics. It was so tight, Jim's knees brushed against the brick walls on either side. Toby followed his best friend, only to get stuck halfway through the alley.

"I can't fit! I can't fit!" Toby wailed, his body sandwiched between the brick walls like so much meat loaf.

But when Bular reached into the alley behind him, Toby's mind changed. He sucked in his belly and pedaled faster. All of a sudden his body budged. Toby started moving forward, putting distance between his back and Bular's claws.

"I can fit," Toby announced. "I can fit! I can fit! Look, Jim, I fit! Awesomesauce!"

Toby made it through to the other end of the alley, reuniting with Jim.

"You did it!" Jim said while hugging his friend.

Bular roared in outrage. All the alleys on this

block were that narrow. There was no way for the evil Troll to reach the humans. He punched at the buildings, shattering their windows but bringing him no closer to Jim and Toby.

The guys took that as a good sign to keep moving. They sped off on their bikes, away from Main Street and away from Bular.

"Man, all of this running for my life is making me hungry," Toby said. "I'm starving!"

"If we live through this, I'll make you sandwiches twenty-four hours a day, seven days a week!" said Jim in return.

CHAPTER 15
FIGHT OR FLIGHT

An hour before the sun set, ambulances brought three gravely injured construction workers to Arcadia Oaks Hospital. As doctors and nurses rushed their battered bodies to the emergency room, the workers raved about being ambushed by some sort of wild animal inside the open sewer trench off Delancy Street. They said it almost looked like a giant black bear, but with horns on its head like a bull. These three workers had managed to escape. Unfortunately, the fourth man in their crew wasn't as lucky.

Doctor Barbara Lake administered anesthesia to all three construction workers and began resetting their broken bones. She focused on healing these poor men, but something they said still bothered her. Delancy Street . . . wasn't that the way Jim and Toby biked home from school?

"Marc, would you mind taking over?" Barbara asked the other ER specialist working beside her. "I . . . I need to check on my son."

"Of course," said Doctor Gilberg, moving over to Barbara's patients. "Everything okay?"

"I don't know," Barbara said, before exiting the emergency room and sprinting to her office to grab her car keys.

"Jim?" Claire called out. "Where are you?"

She had been standing on his front porch for five minutes, ringing the doorbell and peeking between the curtains to see if anyone was home. At first she felt a little guilty about snooping. But, hey, if Jim could hang out outside her house last night, then Claire should be allowed to do the same thing now, right?

Getting impatient, Claire left the porch and circled around the side of the house to the backyard.

"Jim? It's Claire. From . . . um, school?" she said.

Now that the sun had set, darkness covered much of the backyard.

"Are you back here?" Claire asked. "I have some good news I wanted to tell . . . you. . . ."

Claire trailed off when she saw the boulders in the yard. Faint moonlight glinted off them, revealing a couple of deep cuts in each rock. Kneeling down, Claire ran her fingers along the gouges. They looked wide enough to have been made by that fake sword Jim had used as a prop in his audition. At least, Claire thought it was a prop. But if the sword could slice though solid stone, then maybe it wasn't a fake after all. And maybe Jim wasn't all he seemed to be either.

"Who are you?" said a voice behind Claire.

She jumped and saw Jim's mom standing at the door leading from the kitchen to the backyard, a worried look on her face.

"Oh, I recognize you," Barbara said, now that she could see Claire's face. "You're Councilwoman Nuñez's daughter."

"Hi, Doctor Lake," Claire said with an embarrassed wave. "Sorry for, um, trespassing, but I wanted to deliver some good news to Jim in person. He got the part!"

"Part? What part?" asked Doctor Lake.

"Oh, didn't he tell you?" Claire said. "He's going to be Romeo in our school play. Ms. Janeth was totally blown away by Jim's audition. We all were!"

"Wait, wait, wait," said Barbara. "My son was . . . acting?"

"Like a pro," Claire said. "I don't know where you took him for drama lessons, but they really paid off. And that cosplay armor he whipped up for the tryouts—it was so rad."

"Drama lessons? Cosplay?" said Barbara. "Are we talking about the same Jim?"

"*Ay, Dios mío,*" Claire said, slapping her forehead so hard, her shock of blue hair slipped over her eye. "Jim must've been trying to surprise you about being cast in *Romeo and Juliet.* And my big mouth just ruined it. Nice, Nuñez. Real nice."

"Oh, that's okay!" said Barbara, suddenly relieved. "When Jim brings it up, I'll pretend I don't know anything about the play."

"Seriously?" Claire asked while tucking her blue streak behind her ear. "That'd be fantastic, Doctor Lake. Thanks."

"No, thank you, Claire," said Barbara. "I sped over here from the hospital like a maniac looking for my son! He wasn't at school, Delancy Street's a disaster area, and when I came home and only found you here . . . Well, it doesn't matter now. I'm sure Jim is probably off practicing his lines with Toby, safe and sound."

Jim figured he was about thirty seconds away from dying.

Where's Daylight and the armor? Jim's mind raced as fast as his bicycle. *Why isn't the Amulet working? And where can Tobes and I possibly hide that'll be safe from the wrath of Bular? My house? Toby's? Mom's hospital? The Pentagon?*

All these questions cycled through Jim's head as he and Toby stopped just shy of the entrance to their neighborhood. Exhausted and panting after miles of biking at top speed, they needed a moment to catch their breath and think.

"Look at me," wheezed Toby. "Look at me. We're not dead, right?"

Before Jim could answer, he heard movement nearby. Had Bular actually beaten them here?

"Master Jim!" Blinky said in greeting as he emerged from the bushes.

Behind him, AAARRRGGHH!!! tried to camou-flage himself with a few leafy branches that barely covered his enormous form.

"Bular's trying to kill us!" said Jim, his throat dry. "He chased us all over town!"

"And you're still alive!" Blinky said. "I knew you had potential, Master Jim."

Jim threw his hands in the air in frustration. *Kinda missing the point here, Troll!*

"You have a sweet voice," said Toby to Blinky. "But you bring death with you!"

Jim watched as AAARRRGGHH!!! dropped the branches, his muscular body illuminated by the moon-light. He felt a glimmer of hope.

"You guys can fight him, right?" said Jim to the Trolls.

Blinky and AAARRRGGHH!!! looked at each other and burst out laughing.

"I could not hope to possess the skill to defeat Bular," said Blinky, wiping a tear from his fifth eye.

"What about him?" Jim said, still looking at AAARRRGGHH!!!. "He's big."

"Pacifist," grumbled AAARRRGGHH!!!.

"Seriously?" cried Jim, his hope deflating.

How could this day have gone from so great to so horrible so fast? With the one Troll big enough to stop Bular now refusing to fight, Jim would be long dead before *Romeo and Juliet*'s opening night.

"Man, such a waste of a hulking brute," Toby added.

"Thank you," said AAARRRGGHH!!!.

"This is why there is a Trollhunter, Master Jim," Blinky said. "AAARRRGGHH!!! renounced the violent path ages ago, at the Great Rocky Mountain Troll War of—"

Bular's deep roar drowned out whatever else Blinky said. The evil Troll stood at the end of the block, having finally caught up with them. His body heaved from running so far, but he didn't seem nearly as tired as Jim.

"Follow me!" shouted Blinky. "We'll be safe in Heartstone Trollmarket!"

Jim and Toby had no idea what a "Heartstone Trollmarket" was, but it sure sounded a lot better than their current surroundings. They took off on their bikes, following the two Trolls, who ran incredibly fast for their size.

Blinky led them past neighbors' houses, between

parked cars, and around barking dogs. Survival was the first priority. In the few short days he'd known Jim, Blinky had grown quite fond of the boy and wanted to see him live. If any other humans should happen to see their hasty escape this night, well, Blinky would have to deal with those consequences later.

"This way, Master Jim! Master Tobias!" said Blinky. "To the woods!"

Their group cut across Eli Pepperjack's front yard, knocking over some trash cans. Inside his bedroom Eli removed his pathetic cardboard costume just in time to see two monsters with stone for skin dash past the window.

"Yes!" Eli cheered. "I knew it!"

A second later a third, larger and angrier-looking, creature chased them. Eli jumped into his bed and covered his trembling body with his blanket.

"I'm not crazy after all," he whispered to himself. "Those things are real! That can only mean that our fair town of Arcadia Oaks has been overrun with one thing and one thing alone: aliens! Their invasion has to be stopped. And Elijah Leslie Pepperjack is gonna stop them!"

Back outside, Bular trailed after the Trollhunter and his allies. He grabbed a streetlight bearing another missing-person flyer and tore the entire pole to the ground. It triggered a chain reaction, tugging on the power lines that connected all the lampposts on the block and bringing them down around Jim, Toby, Blinky, and AAARRRGGHH!!!.

One of the sparking streetlights landed right in front of Toby's front tire. He slammed into it, and the force sent Toby flying off his bike seat and high into the sky. Fortunately, AAARRRGGHH!!! grabbed Toby in midair. The Troll switched to galloping on all fours like Bular, and Toby held on to AAARRRGGHH!!!'s mossy back for dear life.

They followed Jim and Blinky into the woods, while Bular tripped over Toby's ruined bike and kicked it aside.

"Master Jim!" said Blinky. "Don your armor!"

Jim biked beside Blinky, dodging trees, and said, "I've been trying! The Amulet won't listen to me!"

"Did you speak the incantation?" Blinky asked, troubled by this news.

"I've been incanting like crazy, and it's not working!" Jim yelled.

133

"Just focus and incant, dude!" said Toby from AAARRRGGHH!!!'s back.

The four of them cleared the woods and reached the edge of the dry canal. With surprising grace, Blinky tucked into a ball and rolled down the slope to the bottom of the canal. AAARRRGGHH!!! and Toby lumbered after him, leaving Jim skidding to a halt up top. Normally, Jim would have jumped his bike over the edge and let go of the handlebars for fun. But nothing about this night seemed normal.

Bular bashed through the woods, knocking over trees as he went. With the evil Troll closing in, Jim didn't have room to circle back and build enough speed to jump his bike down the canal.

Jim stepped off the bicycle and removed his helmet. He pulled the Amulet from his book bag.

"Uh, for the glory of Merlin, Daylight is mine to command," said Jim, his voice shaky.

He looked up and saw Bular emerge from the woods, fangs and claws bared.

"For the glory of Merlin, Daylight is mine to command," Jim tried again.

But still nothing happened. No armor. No magic. Nothing.

Bular charged at the unarmed Trollhunter like a deranged bull. Jim had never felt so terrified in his life. Time seemed to slow to a crawl.

Jim thought of Toby, Blinky, and AAARRRGGHH!!! waiting at the bottom of the canal. He thought of Mr. Strickler, who always believed in him. He thought of Steve, who didn't seem so bad compared to Bular. He thought of Claire and how he'd never get to see her dance again. And then Jim thought of his mom and how she would react to losing her only son.

No, Jim thought. *I'm not gonna let that happen.*

As Bular lunged, Jim remembered how Blinky had said the Amulet reacts to the Trollhunter's emotional state. Well, Jim was feeling pretty emotional at this moment. And maybe that was the problem. It was only when Jim stopped overthinking things— like he had during his audition—that he actually felt in control of his destiny.

Jim closed his eyes, emptied all emotion and worry from his mind, and whispered, "For the glory of Merlin, Daylight is mine to command."

He had scarcely finished speaking when Bular hauled back his stone fist and punched James Lake Jr. with all his terrible might.

CHAPTER 16
CUT HIM LIKE A MEAT LOAF

When Jim opened his eyes again, he found himself rocketing high above the canal. Bular's punch had sent him skyward, yet somehow Jim was surprisingly—amazingly—alive. He saw the breastplate and Amulet over his chest and immediately understood that it must have appeared there a split second before Bular had struck him.

It worked, Jim thought with great relief. *Daylight is mine to command!*

As Jim arced downward the rest of the armor formed around his arms and legs in a storm of metal and magic. He landed on his feet at the bottom of the canal, and Daylight appeared in his hand. The night fog cleared, revealing the Trollhunter, ready to fight.

Bular shook his head, still dazed from the shock wave caused when his fist had hit Jim. He boomed out a primal roar so loud it shook the earth beneath him.

"Uh . . . nope," Jim said, before changing his mind and running away.

He ran down the length of the canal, dragging the heavy Daylight sword behind him. Ahead, Toby, Blinky, and AAARRRGGHH!!! waved Jim closer. But Bular landed heavily between them, blocking the Trollhunter's path. Bular roared again, his jaws drooling like a rabid animal's.

Blinky cupped his four hands around his mouth and shouted, "Use your sword, Master Jim!"

Jim's body was exhausted from all the biking and running, but he still managed to lift Daylight and hold it protectively in front of his body.

Bular snorted, unimpressed. "I'll drink your blood out of a goblet made of your skull!"

He ran full-bore at the Trollhunter. Jim's knees felt like they were going to give out, but he kept his ground. Toby saw his best friend's arms quiver under the weight of the sword.

"Cut him like a meat loaf, Jim!" yelled Toby.

Hearing Toby's advice gave Jim a second wind. A wave of energy surged out of the Amulet, down the armor's engravings, and into Jim's arms. Supercharged, Jim swung Daylight and swatted away Bular with the flat of his blade—just as Kanjigar had done in his final battle.

Bular regained his footing and slammed his petrified fist into the canal, cracking the concrete.

"We must work quickly," Blinky said to AAARRRGGHH!!!. "Open the portal!"

AAARRRGGHH!!! rushed over to the canal wall just under the bridge while Blinky pulled that crystal dagger from his pouch.

"The Horngazel," said Blinky, before throwing the object to his Troll friend.

AAARRRGGHH!!! caught the Horngazel, traced a fresh glowing semicircle into the wall, and punched it, activating a new portal.

"Whoa," muttered Toby in astonishment.

Behind him, Jim and Bular circled each other.

Don't think. Become, Jim reminded himself. He silenced the worried voice in his head and stayed in the present, keeping his distance from Bular.

"Master Jim!" called Blinky, pointing at the

portal. "Master Jim, come on! And hurry, please!"

"I'm a little busy here," Jim said, before Bular pulled his twin swords from his back.

"You are not fit to wield the Amulet," Bular spat. "I'll tear the armor off you! Along with your skin!"

Bular swung his blades, but Jim dodged the blow. With Bular's guard down, Jim saw an opening. Channeling his kitchen knife skills, Jim twirled Daylight in his hand and sliced at Bular. Their swords clashed in a shower of sparks. Bular spun around and thrust his swords. Jim parried and struck back. He hacked at the evil Troll over and over again, pouring all his anger and fear into his attack. More sparks sprayed everywhere. Bular deflected the advance with his weapons but struggled to keep up with Jim's increasing speed.

Toby couldn't believe his eyes. Bular actually took a step back. Jim was winning!

"Go, Chef Jimbo!" Toby shouted.

Jim told himself he was back in his kitchen, breaking down a slab of meat with a slightly larger knife than usual. Tightening his grip and summoning all his remaining strength, he drove the blade right toward his enemy's horned head. But Bular saw it coming, and the Trollhunter's sword cleaved instead into his dead stone hand. The edge sank so deep, Jim couldn't pry it loose.

Bular raised his arm, and along with it Jim, still dangling from Daylight's handle. The evil Troll twisted his body powerfully, dislodging Daylight and knocking Jim aside.

The Trollhunter's sword landed twenty feet away and promptly sublimated into a cloud of blue mist. Jim rolled with his landing and sprang back onto his feet, running as fast as he could away from Bular.

Toby, Blinky, and AAARRRGGHH!!! beckoned Jim from inside the portal, which was now closing around them.

"Come on, come on!" Toby said as the canal wall started to reform between them. "Let's go, Jim!"

Jim pushed himself faster, reaching out to Toby . . . but arriving a heartbeat too late. The portal closed, reverting to ordinary concrete once again. Jim lost his balance and stumbled into the wall. The collision rattled Jim's body and broke his concentration. With his distress rising, the armor dissolved into more blue mist, and the Amulet dropped inertly to the ground.

"Oh no," Jim breathed out.

He bent over to retrieve the Amulet and, in doing so, ducked Bular's two thrown swords. The blades stabbed into the wall right where Jim's head had been a moment ago. Startled, Jim saw Bular coming for him, fury blazing in his yellow eyes.

Jim backed into the wall, with nowhere else to go and certain death hurtling toward him. But rather than see his life flash before his eyes, Jim saw a glow spread from behind him. He felt a breeze against the back of his neck that quickly turned into a rushing wind.

With Bular scant feet away, Jim turned around and saw a new portal open from inside the wall. AAARRRGGHH!!!'s massive hand reached out and yanked Jim through the doorway an instant before it, too, closed. Bular careened into the wall, his horns scoring its solid surface. The beast threw back his head and unleashed another deafening howl at the escaped Trollhunter.

"Satisfied?" asked a voice.

Bular spun around and saw Strickler behind him, his hands behind his back and a smug smile across his face.

"Spare me your lectures, Impure," said Bular.

"Oh, I won't say a word," Strickler said.

In the blink of an eye he reverted to his Changeling form and brought his scaly hands forward. They held a Fetch, a spiked stone circle less than a foot in diameter. Bular's savage expression softened into one of fear as he saw a different portal open within the Fetch. On the other side the smoking shadow of a far larger Troll appeared, his one glaring eye fixed upon Bular.

"But I believe someone else wants to speak with you," Strickler added with a self-satisfied smirk.

Bular lowered his head and dropped to his knees before the unblinking stare of Gunmar the Black.

"Father, I—" Bular began.

"Silence," said Gunmar from across the portal. "Even from my exile here in the Darklands, your failure brings me shame."

"I will find the boy!" Bular said. "I will destroy him and deliver the accursed Amulet to you!"

"You will do nothing," said Gunmar, his eye flaring in anger, "unless I allow it. From this moment forward you follow the Changeling's instruction."

Strickler's grin widened, exposing his sharpened teeth.

"He is as cunning as he is untrustworthy," Gunmar said. "And he understands that the best way to destroy a human is not to break his body . . . but to shatter his heart."

"Yes, Father," Bular said so low, Strickler could barely hear it.

"First, you shall oil the Amulet's gears with the Trollhunter's blood," Gunmar ordered. "Then you shall use it to bring about my glorious return so that I may plunge this entire world, above and below, into an Eternal Night. . . ."

Gunmar's dark laughter spilled out of the Fetch and into Arcadia, chilling everything it touched, even a wretch as monstrous as Bular.

CHAPTER 17
I SURVIVED BULAR AND ALL I GOT WAS THIS STUPID AMULET

Jim watched in wonder as his body slipped through the magical path of floating rocks and flickering lights. With impossible speed he zoomed past the Earth's crust, beyond layers of silt, strata, and lava. He felt AAARRRGGHH!!!'s steady hand pulling him deeper, deeper, until the Horngazel portal closed and Jim's sneakers landed on solid ground.

After his eyes adjusted to the darkness, Jim discovered that he had arrived in a cave alongside Toby, Blinky, and AAARRRGGHH!!!. They could still hear Bular pounding against the canal wall, even though Jim estimated there must have been mile and miles of solid rock between them.

"He nearly . . . we nearly . . . he almost . . . ," babbled Jim, still in shock from that close call with

Bular's blades. He took a deep breath.

"Almost what?" asked Blinky. "Speak, Master Jim."

"He almost killed us!" Jim shouted.

"'Almost'! A very important word," said Blinky. "A life of 'almost' is a life of never."

Jim and Toby shared a confused look, then watched the two Trolls move deeper into the cave. They followed Blinky's eyes, which shone like six flashlights in their pitch-black surroundings.

"Why'd the armor suddenly shut off?" asked Jim, stumbling in the dark.

"Master Jim, you are the first human to possess an Amulet crafted for Trolls," Blinky explained. "It's to be expected its behavior will be . . . unexpected."

Right. Unexpected, Jim thought, his head hung low in embarrassment. *Everything about this whole situation is unexpected! How can I be expected to protect others when I can't even save my own life?*

They reached a deep pit in the catacombs. Blinky gestured with his four arms, and a staircase made of crystal steps lit up before them. Jim and Toby leaned over the edge of the chasm and saw the glowing stairs extend way farther underground, in what seemed like an endless spiral. Jim and Toby stared at each other, their eyes wide in shock.

"This way, Masters, this way," said Blinky as he and AAARRRGGHH!!! descended.

"Whoa!" said Toby, testing the first crystal step with his foot. "Are you sure we're safe in here?"

Jim lagged behind his best friend, still replaying the fight with Bular in his head. His body ached with bruises, and his limbs shook as the adrenaline that had coursed through them during the battle now left Jim's bloodstream. But what hurt Jim most was his pride. Slinking down these steps, moving farther and farther underground . . . the whole thing felt like a retreat.

"Indeed," Blinky said, his voice echoing up and down the staircase. "The incantation forbids entry to Heartstone Trollmarket by Gumm-Gumms such as Bular, for they are the most fearsome of Trolls."

"Gumm-Gumms?" Jim asked absently.

"Scary ones," said AAARRRGGHH!!!. He figured it might be a bit too early to tell Jim that, in Trollspeak, "Gumm-Gumm" roughly translated to "bringer of horrible, slow, painful, and thoroughly calculated death."

They reached the bottom of the stairs and entered a new subterranean chamber. Jim took in the bleak stone walls. Nothing grew here. Not even mold.

"Okay, wait, wait," said Jim. "So, Bular can't get in here, right? Into Heartstone Trollmarket?"

Is this where I'll need to spend the rest of my days? thought Jim. *In the dark? Like a coward? Always hiding from Bular so that he can never fulfill his promise of drinking my blood out of a goblet made of my own skull? Is this really how my life is gonna end?*

"No, Master Jim," said Blinky.

He placed his four arms on Jim's shoulders and gently turned him around. Jim's eyes picked up faint, but warm, colors filtering just beyond the very large boulder in front of him. Jim took a step, and then another, moving past the boulder and stepping onto a ledge.

"Wow," whispered Jim, his eyes widening in awe.

Toby stepped behind Jim, and his jaw dropped too.

A massive city spread out before them, glittering like a constellation of underground stars. Its crystalline towers and jewel-studded caves teemed with thousands and thousands of Trolls of all shapes and sizes. For a place this deep below the earth, this hidden from the sun, it seemed so incredibly alive to Jim.

"This is the world you are bound to protect," announced Blinky. "This is Heartstone Trollmarket!"

Jim only looked away from the kaleidoscopic landscape when he felt a strange tickle in his hand. He found the Amulet in his palm and only now realized that he had been gripping it tightly ever since he'd stepped onto the crystal stairs.

Merlin's device pulsed with blue energy.

"Uh, I think this thing's on the fritz again," Jim said.

"Yeah, my cell phone's doing the same thing," said Toby. "The Wi-Fi must be terrible down here."

"Why-Fly?" asked AAARRRGGHH!!!.

"Wi-Fi," Blinky clarified. "It's some sort of electronic force that humans use to share information and adorable pictures of cats—"

"Cats?" said AAARRRGGHH!!!, licking his lips. "Tasty."

"Oh, never mind! Merlin's Amulet does not need Wi-Fi!" yelled Blinky.

Jim couldn't help but smile as his friends continued to squabble, and all those self-pitying thoughts of losing to Bular and running away quickly dissolved. With his mind cleared again, Jim had a new realization. Maybe that battle with Bular wasn't the end of his life. Maybe it was just the start of a whole new one.

Jim faced Toby, Blinky, and AAARRRGGHH!!!, who all smiled at him in relief. Obviously, Jim had surprised them—and himself—by surviving this night. Perhaps he owed it to them—plus all those Trolls down there and all the people above, like his mom and Claire—to try surviving another.

Blinky was right. There may have been many, many champions before Jim, but none of them were human. Judging by the Amulet's unpredictable behavior, choosing Jim had definitely changed the rules of the game. That meant he couldn't ever hope to be like the other Trollhunters, no matter how hard he tried. Jim would have to do this in his own unique, imperfect, and human way.

Tick. Tick. Tick.

The Amulet started ticking in his hand. Its gears clicked in rhythm, matching Jim's heartbeat. Slow. Steady. Confident.

For once, he didn't feel like time was running out. Instead, Jim actually felt like he had more time than ever.

Tick. Tick. Tick.

No more worrying. No more thinking.

Tick. Tick. Tick.

It was time for James Lake Jr.—the Trollhunter—to become.

EPILOGUE
COURAGE REBORN

Kanjigar's eyes snapped open. A black and infinite space replaced the human bridge from which he had just fallen.

Where . . . where am I? Kanjigar wondered.

As if in answer, countless orbs of energy—similar to the ones that once sprang from his Amulet, only larger—appeared out of the darkness and streamed around Kanjigar. The illuminated spheres settled in a wide ring around him and transformed into several ghostly, yet familiar, Trolls in matching suits of armor.

"Welcome, Kanjigar the Courageous," said the female Troll in front.

"Deya the Deliverer?" uttered Kanjigar, recognizing her. "Is that truly you? I haven't seen you since your final battle."

"Your eyes do not deceive you, Kanjigar," said Deya. "You, I, and Merlin's other fallen champions still exist beyond death in this remote afterlife."

"Then this must be the Void," Kanjigar said upon seeing that his own armored body had become transparent and weightless. "And I have joined your Council of Trollhunters."

"I'd almost forgotten how quickly you catch on, Kanjigar. Alas, from this Void, our spirits meet to offer advice, prayer . . . and warning," said Deya.

"Warning?" asked Kanjigar. "To whom?"

Deya stepped aside, revealing another ball of energy. It stretched and flattened into a window of sorts, giving Kanjigar a view into Heartstone Trollmarket. There, he saw his old friends, Blinky and AAARRRGGHH!!!, leading two humans into their sacred land. To make matters more shocking, one of the humans carried the Amulet in his young hand.

"To him," said Unkar the Unfortunate, a small and meek Trollhunter who pointed at the boy with the Amulet. "Take it from me, that kid is doomed! Although he's already lasted longer than I did. . . ."

Kanjigar watched in amazement as Blinky, AAARRRGGHH!!!, and the humans encountered

Draal in Heartstone Trollmarket. Although Kanjigar could not hear what they said, it was plain that Draal believed the Amulet belonged to him, not a human. Draal looked furious, but Kanjigar's spirit swelled with joy at the sight of his son.

Thank you, Merlin, thought Kanjigar. *Thank you for hearing my wish and sparing my son so that he may live a life free of your demands.*

But Kanjigar's heart soon grew heavy when he considered the human with the Amulet. Had Kanjigar's death sealed this boy's fate instead of Draal's?

Over the centuries Kanjigar had seen full-grown Trolls, some triple his size, cower in fear when the Amulet chose them. And yet here was this human child who somehow managed to withstand the Amulet's burden—and Draal's fury—and still keep going.

"Yet I have always known our Amulet to work in mysterious ways, just like its maker," Kanjigar continued. "Is it possible this human will succeed where so many of us have not?"

"Come now, Kanjigar," whined Unkar the Unfortunate. "Surely you don't believe that . . . do you?"

Through the window he witnessed the human enter the Hero's Forge and begin his training under Blinky and AAARRRGGHH!!!'s guidance.

"I do not know," Kanjigar admitted.

The image suddenly shifted to sometime later, showing Draal defending the human Trollhunter and his home from attack. Kanjigar blinked his eyes, and more visions followed. The human's best friend and a female with a streak of blue in her hair now joined the Trollhunter in battle with weapons of their own. Understanding that the Void was showing him glimpses of things yet to come, Kanjigar saw Blinky and AAARRRGGHH!!! guide these humans on adventures under the world and across it. He saw them all grow closer as warriors and friends. He saw them achieve unbelievable victories . . . and suffer a tragic defeat. And through all these wins and losses, ups and downs, Kanjigar saw the human Trollhunter continue growing in skill, confidence, and power.

Kanjigar smiled at the other Trollhunters in the Void and said, "But the very thought of it gives me courage for the future of humans and Trolls alike."

THE BEGINNING

Here's a sneak peek at **WELCOME TO THE DARKLANDS!**

Gunmar the Black howled.

He howled in confusion, unable to tell day from night in this strange new realm. He howled in pain. Ice-cold winds whipped against his body—a body born in the fires of war. And he howled in defeat. Victory had been snatched from his grasp, just as Gunmar had been snatched into these dark lands.

Gunmar forced himself to stand. His hooves nearly slipped on the glowing green rock beneath him, but he found his balance.

Never again will I be brought to my knees, Gunmar promised himself.

He looked out at the Darklands with his single

burning eye and watched his army start to appear around him. One by one, thousands of Gumm-Gumm soldiers arrived in flashes of blinding white light. They, too, crashed against the barren landscape, as Gunmar had done mere seconds ago. They, too, fell over with vertigo and shivered against the sudden cold.

Gunmar turned his horned head upward and saw the portal through which he and his army had been thrown. Killahead Bridge sat atop a jagged stone peak. Its arch shimmered with magic as more Gumm-Gumms plummeted into the Darklands.

Gunmar squinted his eye and stared through the portal. He glimpsed the distant surface world on the other side, as well as the enemy who had just banished him from there.

"Deya," said Gunmar with a low growl.

Deya the Deliverer stood guard at the other end of Killahead Bridge. Her silver Daylight Armor was battered and dirty from weeks of combat, but still unbroken. She planted her broadsword into the battlefield, a grim look of finality in the Trollhunter's eyes. Even across the immeasurable space that separated them, Deya's message was clear: *This war is over.*

RICHARD ASHLEY HAMILTON

is best known for his storytelling across DreamWorks Animation's How to Train Your Dragon franchise, having written for the Emmy-nominated *DreamWorks Dragons: Race to the Edge* on Netflix and the official Dream-Works Dragons expanded universe bible. In his heart, Richard remains a lifelong comic book fan and has written and developed numerous titles, including *Trollhunters: The Secret History of Trollkind* (with Marc Guggenheim) for Dark Horse Comics and his original series *Scoop* for Insight Editions. Richard lives in Silver Lake, California, with his wife and their two sons.